Slide in all Direction

David Laing Dawson

Bridgeross Communications
Dundas, Canada

All enquiries about the motion picture or other
dramatic rights for this book should be addressed to
the author's representative: Gallery on the Bay, 231
Bay St. North, Hamilton, On. marlaise@look.ca

ISBN: 978-0-9810087-1-9

Bridgeross Communications
Dundas, Ontario, Canada

Also by David Laing Dawson

Fiction:

Last Rights

Double Blind

Essondale

The Intern

Non-fiction:

Schizophrenia in Focus

Relationship Management

Film & Video:

Who Cares

Manic

My Name is Walter James Cross

Drummer Boy

Painting with Tom, David and Emily

Cutting for Stone

For Marlaise

1

The wheels of heaven stop

Albert Johannes Wesnicki – whose father had named him right then and there when his mother and aunts were dithering because he wanted either an Einstein or a Brahms, take your pick, and how he'd just been reading that the music part of the brain was very close to the mathematics part, and a long way away from the hockey part – wasn't thinking much about mathematics or music when he staggered out of the crack house at the corner of Barton and Bay on a fine July afternoon in his nineteenth year and lay himself down in the middle of Bay Street North to await the approach of the eighteen wheeler loaded with steel rods that often came fast around the corner this time of day.

Kyle, his good buddy in all things sinful, hesitated but a moment before continuing his loose-limbed journey up Bay Street, muttering over his shoulder, "You stupid bastard, get yourself run over, who gives a shit."

His mother had probably rolled her eyes and shrugged that first day, the way she rolled her eyes and shrugged every time his father told the naming story at the dinner table throughout Albert's childhood, told right after he had announced, a few beer under his belt, "I can talk to the goddamn kid any way I want. I'm the one gave him his name, Goddamnit."

It wasn't much of a crack house, not by world standards anyway. Just a run down rat hole triplex, shifting and sliding in its slow journey down the hill into the lake. On the Barton Street side, one window was tilted a good fifteen degrees and the edge of the roof formed a rather pleasant shallow swoosh instead of the perfect horizontal the original builder had imagined. Kitty corner stood the Bait Shop, carved out of a small defunct Variety store, carrying a few rods and reels, a display case of lures and a few buckets of worms. Where the money changed hands before customers crossed over to the crack house. This was not, thought Albert, where he should be on the day after his father's funeral.

Lying there on Bay Street, he could see the south side of the rat hole triplex, count the missing bricks and think about its one hundred years of decay and slippage. At some point it may have been a decent Victorian two story, maybe housing two or three steel working families, much like his own, before the hookers and dealers took over.

The building would decay and slide and eventually collapse into the lake at a God-like pace and he, Albert Johannes Wesnicki, would decay and slide and collapse into the lake at his own very human pace, but whether the two of them went to the lake or the lake came to them, was merely a matter of perception, and the time it took, was, well, a relative thing. This was, he thought, in his chemical haze, a rather Einsteinian kind of thought. Albert would have smiled to himself at that moment if his lips had not been so dry and if he had had more muscle control around his mouth.

2

It would almost be worth dragging his sorry ass off the pavement, going out to the cemetery, digging up the old man and telling him about his Einsteinian thought. Naw, he could see the way it'd come off. He'd get the hole dug, haul up the coffin, pry it open, and before he managed to tell his story, the old man would rear up, look at the kid he had named Albert Johannes and say, "What the hell, look at yourself, you've pissed your pants." Which would be accurate, though not very Einsteinian.

Several cars had stopped and a couple of people had paused to watch from the corner sidewalk, but no one so far had ventured into the street to take a good look at Albert. Which was not surprising to him. His hair was long and dank, his unshaved chin flecked with vomit, his jacket crusted with spill and city dirt; his pants were wet, and a puddle of liquid spread around him. He would have walked on by himself.

Albert had not wondered, during his childhood, being as naturally incurious about the status quo as most children are, why his father had chosen Brahms when his own taste in music didn't go much beyond Hank Snow, at least not until he and his mother were planning his father's funeral service (and Albert had promised to stay clean and sober at least until the old man was put in the ground) and his mother had said, sitting at the kitchen table, looking older than Albert liked to imagine her, "It has to be Brahms, the music, it has to be Brahms. Your father loved Brahms."

And Albert had said, "Whoa. Just where the hell did that come from? I don't remember any Brahms running through the house. Country and Western, Willie Nelson, maybe."

"He used to sing you kids The Lullaby every night."

"Yeah? I don't remember that."

"Well, maybe only the first year or so. Besides, it wasn't the music. It was the idea of Brahms. He liked the idea of Brahms."

"What the hell is the idea of Brahms?"

"It was....never mind. We'll just have to talk to the organist, that's all."

"You can't play a lullaby at a funeral."

"I don't see why not. Besides, he must have written something else."

And if Albert hadn't run into Kyle the very next day and if Kyle hadn't been holding and if Albert hadn't said to himself, "Okay, sure, just one joint, what can it hurt? After all, the old man's lying in McCall's stone cold, what can it hurt to chill a little?" Then that day would not have folded seamlessly into the next and Albert would have made it to the church in time to hear his mother's sister give a passable rendition of Johannes Brahms' very mellow Ave Maria. But Kyle was holding, and one joint lead to another and then a pipe and then some grey tablets and pretty soon Albert had lost track of time and without the passage of time all commitments and responsibilities become irrelevant, and Albert was able to tell himself that going to the old man's funeral was the last thing he needed right now.

4

"The last frigging thing, the last frigging thing I need right now," he told Kyle, who, not privy to Albert's thoughts, didn't know what he was talking about.

Albert had spent most days the past year either hustling or stoned but he had never before simply lain down in the street and awaited. He'd been to the rat hole triplex at the corner of Bay and Barton a few times before, but this time the guy who lived there on the ground floor was just back from one of his many absences, looking gaunt and wasted. Albert noticed a new motorized wheelchair chained to a railing just outside the door. He had assumed the contraption was stolen, waiting for a buyer, but realized now the guy might actually need it to fetch groceries.

As they'd stepped out of the door into the bright sunlight, Kyle had said to Albert, "He's dying, man. He's fucking dying."

From the sidewalk Albert had looked back over his shoulder at the tall thin man standing half in the shadows of the open door. "How do you know that?" He asked. The man's eyes were looking past them, down the street, or into eternity.

Kyle said, "I just do, man. It's obvious. The guy is dying."

And that was just before Albert lay down in the middle of the road at the corner of Bay and Barton and looked up at the gritty sky loaded with particulate matter, painful memories and uncertain futures, and lay there waiting.

An older man was looking down at him now, a guy from the building being renovated on the other corner. The older man bent over him, and took him by the shoulders, just grabbed the shoulders of Albert's jacket and dragged him backwards across two lanes up over the sidewalk onto a small patch of dry grass and dropped him there. As if the light had changed the traffic began moving. The older man looked down at him a moment, and then stepped back and walked away. A minute passed with nothing new but a single puffy cloud coming into Albert's vision and then Kyle appeared above him and pulled him roughly to his feet, saying, "C'mon man, before the cops get here. Let's go. C'mon."

Albert let himself be righted, turned, and headed down Bay Street toward the Regal Tavern where they could find something cold for his dry, cracked lips.

"Where we going, man?" said Albert.

"Regal," said Kyle.

"Maybe we could swing by the cemetery," said Albert, "The one out by Dundurn."

"Why the hell would we wanna do that?" asked Kyle.

Albert's head was clearing a little. He thought about Kyle's question. "Do you know what the idea of Brahms means?" he asked.

"What?"

"The idea of Brahms. What it means. What it is."

"What?"

"I dunno, man. It's just a thought."

"What's just a thought?"

6

"He wrote a lullaby, y'know."

"Yeah? So?"

"I'm trying to remember it, man. That's all. I'm trying to remember it."

In a surprisingly full tenor, Kyle began to sing, "Lullaby and good night, May the da da de da da."

"That's the one," said Albert.

"It's faggy kind of shit, though," said Kyle.

"The old man was a lot of things, but he wasn't a fag," said Albert, and then after a pause, "The old lady's gonna be some pissed."

"What?"

"I missed his fucking funeral. You believe it? I missed his fucking funeral."

2

There's no one left to torture

The wind blew down the long straight streets and scattered whispers of dry snow across the pavement, along the gutters, touching the concrete walls, and blew the snow and grit up over the city into the lifeless aluminium sky.

Harry was on a mission. Scarf wrapped tightly above his brown Amity coat, kids' woollen mittens on his fingers, beard and whiskers snarled in icicles of snot, he trudged up James, past the oriental grocery, the BiWay and the fur coat place, long dead and abandoned, the little café with potted plants in the window, home to a small Japanese woman, buildings with signs that spoke of a former age of life and commerce. It was early for Harry but he had a long way to walk with the crumpled pages of his poetry in his pocket, a coffee and three pieces of toast in his belly, a dull ache behind his eyes, and, he noticed, one set of laces undone and trailing, which could fucking wait until he came upon a bench to sit his arse upon.

He turned right on Cannon, west, into the harsh wind blowing down the wide boulevard, wouldn't you know it, crossed Bay onto York, leaving behind the core of the city, with its arteries bleeding traffic, the aging heart left behind, warrens for drunks, addicts, derelicts and old poets. Run for it, Harry said to the cars and steel-laden transports grinding by, run for it.

On the upper level bridge, the old viaduct, a grand Victorian entrance to a post-industrial city, Harry paused and raised his foot onto a bench and bent to tie his shoelace. He fumbled with his mittens, took them off, tried again. Straightening up he looked out into Hamilton Bay, on his left the cliffs of Aldershot rising up from the frost-edged lake, crowned with the soft grey mesh of January deciduous and hints of vermilion vinery, and then stretching away on the other side, the coal-black triangles, spires, ribs, plumes, entrails, stacks and orange fires of the old steel mills. Over the entrance to the Bay and the Skyway Bridge an unreachable sun bleached a white nickel into the clouds, but carried no warmth to his face.

Harry carried on through Aldershot into deepest, darkest tree-lined Burlington. He felt uneasy on these manicured streets, with their lying shrubbery, deceitful porches, dissembling portcullis, confabulating thermo-panes. He came to the house eventually, after warming himself in a Tim Hortons. It was a ranch style suburban, fronted by young Scotch pines and a brown wooden fence. He checked the address and paused, before making his way around the side to the back, climbing the three porch steps, and knocking on the door.

A curtain pulled back to reveal a suspicious face. She looked at him without recognition and then closed the curtain. Harry waited. God almighty, he muttered to himself. Do I look that bad? With his coat sleeve he wiped his nose and beard and then knocked again. Again she pulled the curtain back and looked him over more intently. The curtain closed; the inner door opened a crack.

9

"You don't recognize me, do you, Sarah?"

"My God. Harry. What on earth are you doing here?"

"Would it be all right, my sweet, if I answered your question while sitting in your warm kitchen?"

"It is you, isn't it?"

With the door a little more open Harry could see Sarah had put on weight. Her face was rounder, fuller now. Perhaps calmer, and more content. But her eyes had grown dull.

"What do you want, Harry?"

"That's it? What do I want? Not considering an outside chance that I came to give you something?"

"I can see you haven't changed, Harry. I mean apart from the beard and dirty hair and those filthy clothes."

"And you look as fine as ever, Sarah."

Sarah shook her head in the manner of someone watching her new puppy chew on her shoe.

"It is cold out here, Sar, and I've been walking all morning."

She opened the outer door and Harry, after stomping snow off his shoes, slipped in quickly before she could change her mind.

"Nice place you have here," said Harry. He looked at her and then pulled off his shoes with his toes, leaving them on the mat.

Sarah, watching him do this, nodded toward the kitchen table, and said, "You can sit there and I'll make you a cup of coffee, Harry, on one condition."

"What would that be?" asked Harry, already taking a chair.

"That you leave when I tell you to leave. That's all I ask."

"It's what I'm good at," said Harry.

She busied herself with the coffee maker, dumping grinds from an earlier batch, filling the casing with water, the basket with coffee from a black ceramic jar. She didn't speak until she had pressed the 'on' button. "It's been a few years," she said.

"Quite a few," said Harry. He had written poems to her, for her, about her, and they had become eternal, read by young men and women in the first blush of love, or so he liked to think, but could never know. He did know you could sometimes find a collection of his poems on a required reading list at your lesser known universities. While the poems remained young, he could see their muse had not. And yet, in the soft angles where Sarah's neck met her shoulders, and where the small of her back met her hips, and in the tilt of her head as she turned from the window, he could feel the years melt away.

She pushed a mug before him and sat opposite. "Still white, one sugar?"

He gratefully cupped the mug in his hands and nodded. As his body warmed he hoped his clothing would not smell too badly.

"So, I'll bite, Harry. What have you come to give me?'

"A couple of poems, Sarah, in exchange for a warm cup and a gentle smile."

"It's nice to see you being realistic for a change."

"Are you happy, Sarah?"

"I don't think you have the right to ask me that question, Harry. It's an intimate question."

"I don't know about that. It's the answer that might make it intimate."

"Let's see the poems, Harry."

Harry pulled his mittens off, fished two folded sheets of paper from his pocket, and smoothing them as best he could, placed them on the table facing her.

"Could I use your bathroom while you read?" asked Harry, already half out of his chair.

He watched her look up from the table and hesitate. He knew she wouldn't want him going through any other part of her house, the house she shared with a man named Roy. "Did you marry Roy?" He asked.

"What? Yes, of course."

"And the bathroom?"

"Straight down the hall, Harry, on your right."

When he returned he found her still sitting in the kitchen chair, looking a little dreamy, unsettled. He sat and sipped his coffee. She said, "I thought it would be a something new you'd written."

"I found them, buried in a drawer. I'd forgotten where the originals were. I thought they were long gone."

"Am I the young girl in your poem, Harry?"

"You know you are, Sar."

He noticed her eyes were misty when he asked for another mug of coffee, perhaps with a biscuit.

She said, "You better go now, Harry."

"But…"

"It was the one condition, Harry."

Harry was given the biscuit, a few biscuits actually, in a plastic bag to go. He munched on them walking the streets of Aldershot, back over the upper level bridge, this time with the wind at his back. The light snow had stopped, the clouds lifted, the higher sun warmed his face. He veered south on Bay, to the nearer warmth of the Regal Tavern. He used the washroom, and then sat in a corner nursing, into the early evening, a few glasses of beer and some complimentary chips and pieces of sausage. He knew he was avoiding his apartment, which in his mind had taken on a colder, more desolate air, since his visit with Sarah. He watched the regulars come and go, some sitting, like him, for hours. He couldn't quite make out the conversation at the bar, but the cadence of it, the music, the occasional laugh, radiated warmth like dying embers in a hearth. A tall lanky man came in, downed a draft beer, looked around, apparently not finding what he was looking for, and left. An older man, in worse shape than Harry, sat at his beer in the opposite corner, occasionally responding to a conversation no one else could hear.

In the dark, Harry walked the long way back to his room above the coffee house on James North. Still avoiding his loneliness, he walked several blocks out of his way, past the old Custom House sitting above the CN tracks, it's two concrete lions peering at the bushes across the road. It was a deep-windowed, Romanesque building, set back with a grand entrance, built during a time architects believed they could imagine the next century.

Like a wobbling sentry, a lone hooker paced in front of the two lions, bundled up for the cold, looking a little unhappy, and giving Harry only a cursory glance, assuming rightly that he could not help her make her quota. Harry noticed how naked she looked though covered up with leggings and a padded jacket. The red platform heels and bare ankles were exposure enough. While Harry was hurrying by, a van pulled over, and the hooker leaned in the passenger window, negotiated briefly, and then got in. She looked over at Harry just as she opened the door, and smiled at him, a small friendly smile, the kind you give to strangers on foreign soil, acknowledging some commonality.

He hurried on, fighting the cold, somehow cheered by the hooker's smile. Pushed by the wind off the lake he walked up James. The temperature had risen, and turned the ice to slush, but the wind felt more penetrating, colder. At the door to his walk-up he took his mittens off, dug in his pocket for the key. His hand trembled. He couldn't find the keyhole. Harry tried holding his right wrist with his left hand to steady it. It made the movement worse. He took a breath, leaned against the door. Of all the questions confronting mankind, he thought, none is so important as whether or not he had left himself a little in the bottom of the jar. He would have a sleepless night without it. He got the key in and the door opened and he pulled himself up the stairs.

His small apartment was a sordid affair, his only luxury a queen size mattress resting on a box spring. Round shouldered couch,

14

Arborite table, two chairs, grease-stained kitchenette, bathroom with shower stall. And a sea of magazines and books. He got a light on, went straight to the cupboard and found what he had been hoping for. He drank from the bottle, sucking the last drops from the bottom before he sank into the couch, coat still on. In this room he had uncommon moments when, late morning, with two large Styrofoam cups of coffee on the table fetched from the cafe below him, paper and pen in hand, words stumbling from his fingers, he could feel he was in the creative life, when his full concentration was set upon the marks he was making on the paper, caffeine tweaking his neurons, the world around him seeming less ominous, less empty. Perhaps he would work tomorrow.

From his coat pocket he retrieved the slim, near perfect, signed, First Edition he had taken from Sarah's bookshelf on his way back from the bathroom. This book, though not it's contents, was worth, in the right antiquarian bookstore in Toronto, he calculated, maybe ten, twenty bottles of mediocre Scotch.

3

Give me Stalin and St. Paul

"You have a visitor, Wesnicki." She was calling from the other side of the bars, voice just loud enough to rise above the echoing din, the chairs rustling, the random cursing, pleadings, bullshit stuff about soap and tooth paste, and towels, and questions, questions, "Seen my lawyer? S'posed to be in today. Gotta see the doc. Why won't you let me see the doc? That bitch don't give you nothing. What's the use seeing the nurse, you tell me that."

Albert pulled himself off his bunk, clean-shaven, hair short. He left his cell and entered the range, the room of chairs and tables and guys in orange jumpsuits milling about, some of them getting towels for showers, getting toothpaste by reaching through the bars to the high shelf and using it and putting the tube back, some of them busy with papers at the tables, some just standing around, shuffling in the bright light and noise. A few were missing, having their day in court, Albert assumed. The old guy, Herman the German, as usual, was talking and talking, not shutting up, everybody avoiding him, knowing he's nuts, the guy needing some chemicals but refusing to take them. Albert's cellmate was coming toward him, unnecessarily repeating the words of the guard. "You got a visitor, Wesnicki."

His cellmate was baby-faced, young. He'd told Albert he was in for stealing a car. Just took it for a ride, shit like that, he had said. Albert figured there was more to 'shit like that'; a nineteen-year old

16

going for a joyride wouldn't get a few months on Three B unless it was the tenth time and his momma refused to put up bail. He gave the stocky black guy a wide berth, the guy with tight dreads, maybe forty years old, putting in his time, didn't talk to anyone, waiting, just waiting. Most of them were waiting. Waiting for lawyers, psychiatrists, social workers, prelims, bail hearings, sentencing reports, trials, visitors. Jerome was waiting, a lanky skinny guy, late twenties, lost in his orange jumpsuit, but talking up the young guys, telling them he had big plans he gets out, no more bullshit piker stuff, look me up, I mean it, you wanna get in on something bigger. Albert was polite to him, and everybody else, just getting by, man. Sure, I'll look you up, man. No problem.

Five years had passed since Albert had staggered out of the crack house at Bay and Barton and missed his father's funeral. He'd been clean and sober a few times in those five years, held some jobs, and even earned a couple of grade twelve credits by correspondence during one spell his mother had taken him back in after an adequate display of remorse and heart-felt promises. But then he'd get that empty feeling in the pit of his stomach, and sleepless nights thinking about his growing debts to banks, credit companies, dealers, his shrinking opportunities, sometimes rushes of anxiety just walking down the street, and when he had a little money in his pocket he'd always get a call from Kyle or Getty or Jordan, like they always knew: "Hey dude, whassup?"

Now in his twenty-fifth year, Albert had been caught in a drug sweep, a raid on a club on King East, the Zanzibar. An after-hours club with DJ in the basement, money changing hands one floor up, little foil wrappings in a room down the hall from the money room, with the option of sharing with a hooker one flight of stairs above that. He should have known there'd be a raid not long after the body of a meth-withered working girl had been found in the back alley. And he should have tossed his stash, cooperated with the cops. But no, already invincible with amphetamine in his veins, he'd taken a swing at a cop, tried to run, too high to know it'd go all right he just sits and smiles, the way Kyle was playing it. That gave him attempt assault and resisting arrest, on top of breach of probation and possession. His mother had bailed him out once before, swore it was the last time, and kept her word. The judge gave him nine months, reduced to five for the two months spent in lockup before trial, with a year's probation after that, which would take him through December into April. So now he was wintering over in the Hamilton Detention Centre. Half of the guys in here were just wintering over, waiting for the spring.

When he got to the bars of the sliding gate between the range and the station, the screw named Laura told him again, "You got a visitor, Wesnicki, might wan' a brush your teeth."

"Is it a pretty lady?"

"You wish." She let him out with her large key. Some of the younger inmates hovered around the briefly opened gate like zoo animals at feeding time, as if a miracle might happen, pizza or marijuana being delivered, announcements of pardons for all, news from home. Laura pushed them back with a simple glare. Albert joined a few other orange suits in the outer cell in front of the guards' station, guys waiting for the nurse with the medication wagon, or escorts for some work detail. He glanced at a couple of the guards on the other side of the Plexiglas watching their monitors. He waited patiently while Laura unlocked the larger of the two bare rooms the lawyers used, for an older woman in dark suit and sensible shoes with bible under her arm, Official Visitor tag on her lapel. Three of the orange suits followed the woman into the room, taking seats fastened to the floor around a wooden table, ready to receive the word of the Lord and be led away from sin and temptation. Albert had signed up for a few of these sessions, anything to get away from the random noise and bullshit of the range. He liked the art history lady best. You could keep the religious crap. What a sight though, four, five guys in half-zipped up orange jumpsuits, all of them tattooed up the wazoo, two of 'em at least can't read or write, listening intently to this sweet gray-haired old lady showing them pictures in her art books, barely able to hear above the constant echo in the place. They were all waiting for glimpses of nudes, really, and one day she tells the one guy who showed up, that next week she's going to bring a masterpiece that turned art on it's head early last century, something called "Nude Descending a Staircase", by a French dude named Duchamp, which was why she had seven guys crammed into the room seven days later, including Albert, Jerome, and the black guy who didn't talk. They're all leaning forward, almost drooling in anticipation, when she opens a large book and shows them this fractured oil painting all lines and angles and planes, you could barely make out the legs, ten of them at least, coming down some

19

stairway, and no tits at all, least he couldn't see any, and sure no beaver no matter how hard they stared.

Albert was thinking, this'll sure keep the boys away from sin and temptation, but the guys in orange were probably thinking about how long till their next smoke and the old lady was sniffing, cause there wasn't much circulation in the little room and these guys had worked up a sweat just thinking about 'Nude Descending a Staircase'.

Albert was led off the Three B Unit and taken down the elevator by a screw named John, who handed him over to another guard on the main floor, who took him to the visiting area down the hall and locked him in. John, who didn't smile once, took two other orange suits as well, and continued down another floor to put them to work in the laundry. It all looked the same in here, hard to tell north from south, east, west. Signage was minimal. Nothing helpful like, "This way to the Exit." The art lady told him she orients herself by thinking CAB backwards when she gets off the elevator on the third floor, which meant B range was to the left, C to the right, and A straight ahead, except straight ahead was a wall you had to go around, all of which struck Albert as A. overly complicated, and B. more evidence of having too much time on his hands if he's actually thinking about this shit.

He knew who'd be waiting on the other side of the Plexiglas barrier with the speaking slots. He could dream a little, tell his cellmate it was one of those Hollywood babes recently come available, but apart from his lawyer, the only person who'd stand in line outside the main door, tell the intercom she was here to visit inmate Albert Wesnicki to whom she was, unfortunately, related, go through the metal detector for

20

him, take her belt off, maybe her boots, put her car keys and purse on the tray for inspection, was his mother. His lawyer might bypass the lineup, but his mother would have to stand on the sidewalk waiting with the pregnant, tattooed, and pierced girlfriends, reluctant fathers, dope smuggling brothers, the Sally Anns, the fundamentalists, Evangelicals, Baptists, all the guitar playing Messengers of God, waiting to be buzzed in to do good work. He never understood the girlfriends visiting, their guys having already demonstrated they were not good marriage material. But the true believers, he knew, loved a captive audience.

She was there, waiting for him. Though she hadn't come to court for him, not since the first couple of times, she did visit the Detention Centre once a week. A year after his father's funeral, when they actually spoke of it briefly, he had told her that he'd been too sick to come; he'd gotten food poisoning off something. She'd said the only thing making you sick is the shit you put up your nose. He tried, "You wouldn't have wanted me there anyway, mom. I might have gotten up and said something tha'd spoil the occasion. I might have told the truth."

She had said, "The truth would be good once in a while."

He'd said, "You gotta expect lying, mom. Once you're into the drugs you gotta lie. There's no choice. Lying's like breathing when you're addicted. It's all part of the illness."

"Jesus Murphy." She had said. "You do talk such a line of bullshit." On the anniversary of his father's death she'd let him take her to the cemetery, and then for a coffee at Tims. Not showing for the

21

funeral was unforgivable, she had told him, but they had to go on, and he was her son, after all, God help her.

He took a chair opposite her, smiled, waited to be asked, "How are you managing?" Instead she said, "Your sister's getting divorced again."

He said, "What? She's only been with this guy, what? Two years?"

"You could be a big help to her, you know, if you weren't always in trouble yourself."

"C'mon mom. That's not fair. She's the one moved to B.C."

"And you're the one in here."

"Yeah, look." He didn't know what else to add he hadn't said before. "You doing okay, mom, I mean getting out at all, anything?"

"Regular party girl."

"Hey, I only got a couple more months. This time I swear, I'll come by, I'll help you fix the place, I swear to God, I'll stay clean this time."

"I don't need your promises, Albert."

"No, look, I've been doing a lot of thinking. I mean it. I've been pissing away my life. It'll be different this time. I haven't used anything in three months."

"You're in jail. You haven't been able to."

"You can get anything in here, mom, you'd be surprised. I'm clean because I decided to get clean."

"Albert. I don't need to hear it. Really. It's up to you. You want

22

to clean up, stop using drugs, you do it for yourself. Not for me, not for anybody else, not because you have to, but because you want to."

"Straight out of the Al Anon playbook, right?'

"It's been helping. I should have gone long ago, maybe learned to deal with your father better."

"I should have made it to the funeral. I'm sorry. I am sorry about that. I swear to God I am."

"Albert, you're my son, really, now wait a minute. What I'm saying is that won't change; I'm always going to stand by you, but from now on what you do with your life is up to you. I'm not carrying it no more. I'm just not up to it. I can't keep caring. It's too hard. That's all there is to it." A tear formed in her eye. She brushed it with her hand, said, "I hate coming here. I hate it." And then without saying goodbye, without looking back, she got up and left the visiting area.

On his way back to Three B, once again escorted by the silent guard John, Albert felt sorry for himself. He knew this was a dangerous state of mind to be in. He'd be vulnerable to the guys selling their pills, or the small packets smuggled in by their girlfriends.

"She bring you any smokes?" asked Jerome, as Albert stepped back into the bright lights and noise of the range.

He wanted to hit Jerome, smack him in the face. Not sure why, maybe for his mother. And that was the moment he realized he felt worse for his mother than for himself. It was a start.

4

Nothing you can measure anymore

She didn't visit after that. Instead she sent him a postcard each week, something you could buy in any variety store in the region, featuring Dundurn Castle, or Niagara Falls, Queenston Heights, the battle of Stoney Creek. A different Ontario location each time, with the same inscription, a simple, "Wish you were here."

It did make him smile, his mother's wry sense of humour, and her not giving up on him, not yet. He phoned a few times but she didn't pick up. He guessed her call display showed either 'unknown caller' or 'Ontario Government', which meant if it wasn't her son, it was either someone selling something or the taxman. She could do without talking to either.

But he couldn't go five months without talking to someone, and although Jerome could be a pain in the ass, he was probably the least dangerous of his choices. You had to keep some distance from the ball grabbers, the dealers, the psychos, the guys needing Anger Management, and the sex offenders.

Albert could read one of the well-used paperbacks lying around the range, old stuff by Frank Slaughter or Pearl Buck, or lie on his bunk staring at the ceiling, attend some of the gospel meetings, ask to visit the doc, tell him he couldn't sleep, but he knew the doc wouldn't give him anything good, just one of those pharmaceuticals that kept you doped up all day, or he could sit and listen to Jerome, the guy a bullshitter but told a good story. In fact, Jerome seemed incapable of answering any question in a single sentence, everything turning into a long story. Which was okay. Albert had time to listen.

So one long afternoon putting in his time, waiting, he asked Jerome what he was in for, and instead of simply 'breach of probation' he got this story:

"It all started with Frank, Frank saying, 'You see that. I leave her for five minutes she's hitting on some other guy.'"

"Who the hell is Frank?"

"Just a guy I knew. Had a small grow-op, trying to get into something bigger. He's talking about his woman, calls herself Jasmine, you ask me though her real name's probably Shirley."

"Okay, so Frank sees his woman Jasmine Shirley hitting on some other guy."

"Right. We're waiting on her outside the liquor store. We can see her through the big windows in the front, and I say to him, 'Frank, it don't mean a fucking thing. You take a look at that guy? She's just doing her thing.'

"It's one of those situations you know you should have kept your mouth shut. Frank turns on me, says 'What'd'ya mean, doing her thing?'

"I tell him he should know. He says, 'No. I don't fucking know.'

"I tell him to forget it.

"But he's crowding me now. He's short but tough. He says, 'You got something to say, you say it. You say it to my face.'

25

"And I know this is not a good place to be, standing outside the liquor store at the Shelburne Mall in Oak Bay trying to point out a few facts of life to a jealous man."

"Hold it," says Albert. "Where the hell's Oak Bay? And why're you outside the liquor store waiting on Jasmine?"

Jerome is distracted for a moment by an argument in the far corner of the range, something about fucking with the toothpaste as far as he can make out. Then he explains to Albert, "We don't wanna get caught on camera, Frank or me, and Jasmine is the one wants the bottle."

"Okay, what about Oak Bay?"

"Oak Bay's in Victoria. West coast, man, and it ain't Hamilton, you get what I mean."

"What were you doing out there?"

"I'll get to it. You gotta have patience. You gonna learn anything you do time, it's patience."

They were sitting side by side at a picnic table, on benches, all one piece, bolted to the floor. You couldn't tell what kind of day it was outside, the small windows high and looking out at nothing. Jerome was right. If he had anything he had time. Albert shifted to a more comfortable position, his back to the table, settled in to hear Jerome's story in Jerome's way.

Jerome said, "Okay, you wanna hear what happened?"

"I'm ready. I got all day. "

"Okay. So I'm in the Regal, minding my own business."

Albert says, "We're back in Hamilton now?"

26

"Right. Hamilton. I haven't been out of the joint more than a few weeks, got nothing going on. I'm amusing myself watching a couple of old ladies sitting at the bar, you know the kind, blue-rinse hair, costume jewellery, looking out of place, a fat hooker sitting between them, having a good time talking up a storm. Can't figure what they got in common, less the old ones are semi-retired working the nursing homes, back for a class reunion.

"That's when Frank come over, right when I was trying to figure out the old ladies. I know him but I don't know him, know what I'm saying. He takes a chair, right away starts telling me how nice Victoria is in the summer, all these well heeled citizens hungry for a little product. I don't know where he's taking this. I figure he knows I'm only out of the joint a few weeks, probably got nothing going on, and I know he's gonna pitch me some hair-brained thing. Some big score he's got lined up. Tells me he and his woman Jasmine are gonna drive out in the van. Tells me they got a friend in Victoria they could hole up with for a while. The guy has his own lab, he says. Big opportunity there, he tells me. Lots of money around, the weather's always good, and the cops are slow. Tells me they don't even carry guns, which I learn later might have been true fifty years ago, but not now. Tells me some of the best Cannabis is grown right on the island these days, and not so many bikers to contend with. He orders a couple of beer, one for me, one for himself. I notice the old ladies are leaving, not giving me a chance to figure them out. He waits till I've finished the beer before he gets to the point. He has enough weed in the van to make the journey, needs a little help with gas, and he doesn't fully trust this lab guy, so a partner might help. Tells me I got no muscle on me but I can look pretty scary being so tall."

Albert says, "You're on probation at the time, right?"

"Sure, of course. But the deal's sounding pretty good. The guy's got the lab, we bring him the raw ingredients, sell the product, provide a little protection, enjoy the smog-free Pacific air. The mark-up's the thing gets to me. You know what it is? Ten. Ten times. Turn cocaine into crack and mark it up ten times. Nothing else you can do that with."

Albert, looking up high at the window, says, "Bottled water."

"Yeah, okay, bottled water. But you got big start up costs there."

Albert looks in Jerome's direction, sees him seriously considering bottled water. He says, "Back to the Regal."

"Okay. So I go for it. Got nothing else going on. Packed my bag. Next morning I'm in the van with Frank and Jasmine.

"Took us four days to get to the west coast, stopping two nights in cheap motels, driving through the other nights. It's a new Dodge van, pretty clean, so I figure it's probably hot, but what the hell, I'm just a passenger, right? This Jasmine, she's got a nice smile, good set of tits, Olive skin, part black I figure, all the right curves but nothing too big. One night I'm driving, Frank's asleep in the back, Jasmine up front her job to keep me awake, we're on the Trans Canada, doing one twenty, one thirty past Regina, she lights up a joint, puts it in my mouth, then lets her hand drift down to my crotch and she gives me a little squeeze.

"It's pretty clear what she has in mind there, with her boyfriend asleep in the back seat, but I figure just my luck she'll have my cock in her mouth, we'll hit a bump, Frank'll wake up and I'll find myself standing at the side of the road in nowhere Saskatchewan trying to hitch a ride minus one dick. I hesitate for a minute but she's got me hard now so I unzip my fly, which ain't easy while you're driving le'me tell ya, and Jasmine gives me the sweetest blow job on the prairies. Yeah.

"When Frank wakes up and takes over the driving, she probably does the same for him, and then in Alberta, the sun coming up, I got the wheel again, and again Jasmine's keeping me awake, this time just giving me a hand job cause Frank's dozing in the back, not snoring yet."

Albert says, "We ever gonna get to B.C. with this story or you gonna relive every blow job on the way?"

"Sometimes," says Jerome, "The journey's more important than the destination."

"At this rate I'll be back on the street before I find what happened at the liquor store."

"Thing is about Victoria, it's got money all over the place, a shack's worth maybe half a mil, the same thing here you might pick up for sixty grand, I kid you not. But it makes you uneasy, all that fresh air, people walking their poodles, cars stopping for pedestrians. I'm feeling, how d'ya say it? Like a fish out of water. Even Jasmine's blow jobs don't make up for it. Besides, she's hanging onto Frank pretty tight now, letting me know that was just her way of getting through the prairies. Then the lab turns out to be a set of scales, a sink and a Bunsen burner in a rented split level in the suburbs. Frank's friend, the chemist, nowhere to be seen. Frank gets us in through a basement window, and we wait for the guy but he doesn't show. Frank figures someone capped his ass, but I figure by the look of the place he's just gone offshore to bank his money.

"We smoke up, go through the guy's liquor cabinet, sit around, watch a few movies on the big screen TV, a little porn, but you know how shitty that is, a few minutes into it Frank and Jasmine head off to a bedroom and I'm left to do myself.

"We've spent three days like this, sitting around waiting for the guy, arguing about how to raise some money to buy product, to buy enough cocaine to turn into enough crack to make a profit, after using some ourselves, in a city we don't know, I mean do we knock off a seven-eleven, then pick the first scruffy looking guy in a rough part of town and ask him if he's holding? Gimme a break. So far we haven't seen any rough parts of town, though I know there's gotta be some. I'm saying maybe they don't do drugs out here, you see 'em all jogging and sitting in sidewalk cafes drinking Starbucks, doing some Tai Chi thing in the park. Frank says that's just the surface, man. He says underneath they're as fucked as anyplace. He's been toking he gets a little philosophical. Says just the opposite is true. They're all running so fast from shit and death they'd love a little fountain of youth. It's about that time when Jasmine gets real bored by it all and says they have to go get some booze or she's gonna fucking die. Says it like that. I'm gonna fucking die.

"Which is why Frank and me are standing outside the liquor store in the Shelbourne Mall, Jasmine's inside flirting with some gimp, and me and Frank are having this intense discussion."

Albert says, "Finally. I thought you were never gonna get there."

"Wesnicki!"

Albert turns toward his name being called by a guard outside the gate. The guard's holding a towel and soap, means it's his turn for a shower. He turns to Jerome, says, "It's been three days, man. I'm gonna have my shower, come back clean."

"You don't wanna hear what happened?"

"Yeah, sure. But I won't smell so bad. Be able to concentrate more. You can re-visit all those blow jobs while I'm gone."

Albert came back in the same orange jumpsuit but a fresh pair of jockeys, thinking how much he's going to appreciate simple things like soap and hot water and clean underpants he gets out. Jerome was still sitting there, eyes half closed, like he'd taken Albert's instruction to heart.

Albert sits beside him, Jerome sniffs, goes back to his story, says right off, "The thing is I figure we could have this conversation, Frank and me, no problem, we were outside the Regal or most other joints in Hamilton two in the morning. Wouldn't matter it ended up with two drunks shouting and pushing at one another. But it's seven in the evening in Oak Bay. We stand out, man, among the well-heeled citizens parking their Mercedes and BMW's and going in for single malts and Old Speckled Hen. But I'm beginning to regret leaving

31

Hamilton where I could always figure some way to score. Frank's in my face telling me to come out with it, say my piece. So I tell him. I tell him Jasmine's just a fucking tease, man. Look at the guy she's playing. He's a gimp for Christ's sake. She's just setting him up.

"Frank steps back, interested now. He says, 'Setting him up for what?'

"I tell him, 'For a fall, man. You know – she makes him think she likes him, then she sticks it to him and walks off.' I'm thinking about her doing me and then shrugging me off, but I'm not stupid enough to tell him that. He says, 'What the hell does that get her?'

"I tell him, 'She's your woman, man. I'm not saying any more.'

"And he asks me, 'You figure she's setting me up too?'

"I'm watching the people coming from the Shoppers' Drug Store and going into the liquor store. I try to get him off this topic. I tell him, 'Look at the good citizens. First they get their Percs, their Oxies, now they need something to wash 'em down?'

"But Frank's gnawing at this bone. He says, 'I asked you a question, man.'

"I tell him, 'You're in love with her, for Christ's sake. There's no reasoning with a man in love.'

"And he says, right out, 'You think she's a whore?'

"And it's one of those moments you know, a guy should reassure another guy, tell him what he wants to hear. But no. I'm bored with the scene. I tell him, 'There's no fucking thinking about it. She is a whore.'

32

"Now I got six, seven inches on the guy, but he's all muscle. So when he takes a swing at me I know it's gonna hurt, but the thing I'm thinking is, the inevitability of it all, you know what I mean. Like here we are, on the west coast, gonna make some big money, and I'm about to get knocked down in a parking lot. It's like when I was seventeen and this guy I was hanging with said he needed some money and why not do the Mac's Milk across from the park, nothing to it, and nobody cares we take a few bucks. And at the time I knew this was not a good idea, not a good spur of the moment idea anyway, and I gotta admit I was not altogether surprised when the guy pulled a knife in the store, and got the two of us charged with armed robbery when the cops caught up with us. Thing is from the moment I began hanging with this guy it was inevitable I'd be charged with armed robbery. And then put on probation on account it was my first serious offence, followed by breach of probation. Like day following night."

Albert says, "So Frank punches you out in the parking lot."

Jerome gets back to his story. "Naw. It was a glancing blow. The guy didn't have much reach. And right at that moment, Jasmine comes out the swing door carrying her fucking bottle, I'm holding my jaw, and I'm saying to Frank, 'You know what your trouble is, man? You know what your trouble is?'

"'Hey sweetie.' Jasmine was saying to Frank, taking his arm. And I'm doing that thing you do when you're pissed at yourself, you know, I'm yelling at him but I'm really yelling at myself. I tell him, 'Your fucking trouble is…is you think you're in control. You think you can decide something. You think you got choices. You'd be a happier man you just let shit happen. You know what I'm saying?'

"Like I said before, outside the Regal there'd have to be a fair quantity of blood on the ground before we'd hear the sirens. But this was Oak Bay. So sure enough I hear that ominous little 'whoot' sound as a cruiser pulls into the parking lot. It was inevitable. And then two cops getting out of the cruiser and coming over slowly. It's playing out just the way it should. I figure they'll come over and address us each as 'sir', but they'd have ample cause to search and they'd find both of us holding a little weed and Jasmine would make like she didn't know either of us, and we'd be taken to the back seat of the cruiser and hafta hand over our I. D. s and the cops would run them through their computer and a lot of priors would show and maybe an outstanding or two, and they'd take us down to the station and maybe tap into CeeFiss and I don't know what they'd find on Frank but they'd find me in breach in Ontario. That's the way I figured it would play, but then the radio in the cruiser crackles and the cops turn back to answer it, keeping one eye on the small crowd and me and Frank standing still, and they answer the call, and then suddenly they get back in the cruiser, put the bubble on the roof and pull out fast with the siren wailing, going to something far more important than two scruffy drunks making a scene in front of a liquor store.

"And I'm thinking, well now. Nothing's inevitable after all. Frank's ignoring me, but Jasmine comes by, says, a little flirty, 'C'mon Jer. Let's get out of here before they change their minds.'

34

"But you know, that's when I'm thinking, do I need this bullshit? Sitting around waiting for the chemist, who may never show. I got choices to make. I could go with Frank and Jasmine. I could ditch Frank and Jasmine. I could rob the liquor store while the cops are busy. Or I could catch the nine o'clock ferry to Vancouver and head back east, pick up some easy money in Calgary on the way, and find some action back home. The cops getting called away was some kind of omen, telling me something. This ain't your city. Go back to Hamilton."

Albert says, "That's the thing about omens. You gotta know how to interpret them. Me, I'd a thought that meant I was in the right place. Cops can't see me, sort of Star Warsy: 'These aren't the droids you're looking for.'"

"Yeah? Maybe. Cause I figure I'll come back to a city I know, which I do, but my PO's a prick, and the judge gives me a few months in the joint for breach. So maybe you're right, but I figure the whole thing's a message. I been letting other assholes decide my life, know what I mean, good ole Jerome, gets talked into anything. So this time I get out, I'm making my own plans, no Franks or Jasmines in them. My idea, my plan, my score. Something big. No more small shit."

Albert says, "So you got busted for breach. Had the opportunity to settle down in beautiful Victoria with the blow-job queen, sell a little product to keep yourself rolling in big Macs, and you come back to Hamilton."

"That's about it."

"I guess home is home, not much you can do about it."

35

That night Albert wakes to the sound of his cellmate in the lower bunk whacking off. It's going to be a long winter, he thinks, and he tells himself he's damn sure he's not gonna make this place his permanent home.

5

Feel the devil's riding crop

Rock solid putrid green fluorescent eye sore corridor straight to the end, walking carefully, tilting left to the wall, coming up to the line, three before him, one fat crying woman, one fuzzy vague anxious man, one angry short-haired butch girl arms carved up, uncovered messages. Metal cart of pills and Dixie cups, the nurse saying, "Your turn, Harry." And Harry waiting, waiting until the fat woman had left a clear passage, and then taking the last three steps to the metal cart. Early morning pill parade, it was. The nurse saying, "Hold out your hand, Harry." And giving him a tiny cup of salts and minerals and vitamins, and then a tiny cup of two Lithium tablets, and then a tiny cup of one Effexor XR red and black capsule, and then a tiny cup of a tiny white Ativan, and Harry swallowing each with a swig from a larger Dixie cup of water, one after the other going down and lying heavily on his empty stomach. She said, "Your hands are pretty steady this morning."

He looked at them, involuntarily spreading the fingers. "Not so bad," he said.

"Jesus, Lord, Boyo. You waiting for a bus?" The guy stepping in line behind Harry, a displaced Newfoundlander, Donny, prone to wearing muscle shirts over his short, stocky, fifty year old chest, sometimes riding up over his belly. "My nerves is shot," he said past Harry to the Nurse. "You thinks you can up the dose a little, darlin'?"

Harry stepped aside and watched Donny look down with disdain at the little cup of pills the nurse handed him. "Lord Jesus," he said. "Not enough here to calm a lobster in heat."

Brothers of the bottle, Harry and Donny knew one another instantly, though Donny couldn't read or write and brought his letters and forms over to Harry to read for him. "Never learned," was as much of an explanation as Harry ever got. But the man, by God, had a poetic way with the spoken word that Harry almost envied. Although, thought Harry, maybe you can either envy or not envy, with no room for almost envy.

On the soft triangle between his left thumb and forefinger, Donny had five ink tattoo spots, each for a year in Federal, Kingston or Moncton. "Jesus Lord, I was drinking pretty good those days, in fights all the time. Spent most of my teens and twenties in one lockup or t'other. Nothin' serious though, aggravated assault, attempt, that kinda bullshit."

Donny was convulsing when they brought him to the hospital, withdrawal from Valium, he told Harry, bin as high as eighty milligrams a day, but they no sooner got that fixed up, he goes into D.T.s. "Lord love ya, had crawlies all over me. And then they got that over and the nerve give out. Not one ting, it's ta-other. But I never went near the crack. That cracks real bad. Seen what it did to my old buddy Dave."

Harry was acquainted with the Delirium Tremens, though usually he could count on somebody bailing him out before the worst of it turned him into a muttering monstrosity, cowering in the closet.

The signed first edition, worth more than he expected, had got him through until early March, but he wasn't doing any writing. He'd have the pen out, the paper, the coffee cup, and he'd want a drink, just a little, get the right chemical balance, a little excited, not too excited, focussed but not too focussed. He'd run out of money and booze about the same time he decided to go cold turkey, get clean, look up his daughter, maybe even talk to his old agent. Resolution forty-nine in which the party of the first part agrees with the party of the first part to get clean and lead a productive life. But mainly because he'd run out of booze and money.

Day one proved a wash out. Wanted to sleep all the time. Day two and three were good, not sleeping, always thirsty, having to piss hourly, but writing, a couple of poems good as anything he'd done before, beginnings of a short story, maybe a novel, going all night when he couldn't sleep. Day four and five it was getting rough, his mind on the verge, on the edge, his body full of electricity, couldn't sit still, couldn't hold the pen, doodling weird little creatures with long crooked legs, and then these drawings of his beginning to move about the page on their own, and him pulling back, knocking the chair over, balling the paper and throwing it, and then throwing his cup, and then his chair, and then knowing he wasn't going to make it, wasn't going to get through this, felt the edges of his brain scraping against his skull, felt the pit of despair beckoning, felt like decking the halls of Bedlam, becking the balls of Hedlam, his brain looping and his eye deceiving, and then, overcoming an outrageous fear of stepping in the puddles of linoleum light, leaving his own kitchen and going down the lonely hall

39

banging on each apartment door until some skeleton sticks his head out and says, "What the fuck you want?"

But Harry finds he can't say what he wants, his words a bad salad of poems and songs and the current price of eggs. He slumps to the floor next to the skeleton's door, the thin man stepping out to look at him.

Harry looks up at the man, finds the man's head is aglow from the light behind him, his image watery, and at his feet the snakes scurrying.

The man looks down at Harry, seeing him clearly there, not well, asks, "Is there anyone I can call?"

"I'm all right," says Harry, brushing ants off his shoulders, out of his eyes, the ants trying to reach the portals of his ears.

'No, you're clearly not," says the thin man.

Harry tries to get his wallet out, spilled papers, old Kleenex, receipts, cards on the floor. He points to a small yellow card between his legs. "That's my daughter," he says. "Phone number. Probably working."

"It's Saturday," says the thin man, picking up the card, looking at it, then returning to his apartment, leaving Harry with his ants.

The ambulance took him to the Emergency of St. Joseph's Hospital where they gave him an I.V. with minerals and salts, and Dilantin, and loaded him up with zeens and zines until he slept a while and finally wakened, knowing where he was, and the year and the month, if not exactly the day, and the ants were gone, and he could

40

almost hold a fork steady enough to feed himself. They were going to discharge him then, send him home with Dilantin and Ativan and a card with the AA number to call, when his daughter talked to the head of his old department at the University, who called somebody at the hospital, and they took another look at Harry, seeing him now maybe not as a street drunk, but an alcoholic with underlying mood disorder, as he heard the intern put it, now calling his reckless trysts with the bottle, "self-medicating". Harry had always understood the power of words, and these words got him sent to the Psychiatric Hospital rather than the Mission or the Sally Ann. He especially liked the concept of "underlying mood disorder" as it resonated with "a demon in the undergrowth", and the assumption that went with it, that is that he drank, not from cowardice or shame or even pleasure, but from an honest attempt to doctor himself, to treat the illness within, the demon in the undergrowth. He went without protest, knowing he would not be the first, nor the last poet to be thus directed.

A nice Irish doctor at the hospital on the hill found even more precise words to describe Harry. Bipolar Type Two, he called it, having ascertained that Harry, on occasion, might feel happy, enthralled, exhilarated, and not always weary. His daughter, having gone so far as having Harry redefined medically, and placed in safekeeping, did not visit. "I won't visit," she had told him. "The place creeps me out. But if you, you know, stay sober afterwards, we'll see."

It was enough for Harry. She had, he thought, forgiven him running off with Sarah, and leaving her mother, and the rather public thing he'd had with another young woman. She had said to him then,

"Dad, you can go with any woman you want, but if I catch you with someone younger than me, I'll kill you." She was in her mid-thirties now, two children, a good husband, a very stable life, as she pointed out to him, contradicting his predictions of human behaviour.

So now in safekeeping for a few weeks of early spring, he paced the halls, he listened to Donny, he watched; he told himself there was material here. He let the lithium dull his locus ceruleus, clog the band width of his corpus callosum, slow the binaries of his temporal lobe. He let his body heal from the excesses inflicted upon it, knowing all the while that once back in his den above James Street, he would.....

"Lord love a duck," said Donny, sitting down beside him in the day room, the featureless open space encircled by well-used chairs. "I gotta be honest wit ye. I did try the crack once, when I couldn't get no Valiums. It just grabs you by the balls, the crack does, and it don't let go. The one time I done it though, I busted my ankle, never healed proper. Wasn't really the crack that done it, though. I fell off a whore is what did it. She was a plump round thing. Nothing much to get hold of, you get my meaning. Never did heal proper."

It was mid April by the time they discharged him back to his apartment above the coffee shop on James. He had attended group, an AA meeting or two, taken his pills, had a haircut, his beard trimmed. He had watched the early April rains through the mesh on the windows of the day area, the first daffodils and irises emerge in the sparse gardens on the grounds. At night he had slept deeply, medicated. Donny entertained him until Donny was caught smuggling in a bottle

42

and then unceremoniously discharged with the address of the Mission printed on a small card.

Harry's rent had been paid a month in advance and the hospital kept him just short of a month. Nobody seemed to have noticed he was gone. The cab let him off after doing a 360 at the Shoppers Drug on the opposite corner. With a paper bag of his few things, standing on James, he noticed a new name on the small panel of buzzers: Wesnicki. The apartment next to his own. He speculated that this Wesnicki could be a failed poet like himself, or a young man sponsored by the John Howard Society, or a man in mid-life punishing himself for leaving his wife.

Once in his apartment, Harry sat briefly in each of his chairs, then for a while in the tattered armchair in his small cluttered living room. His phone didn't ring. There were no messages from Sarah or his daughter. In the bathroom he flushed all but his sleeping pills, and then left his apartment and walked, on this fine spring day, to the liquor store.

6

Say it clear, say it cold

The old man was sprawled on the kitchen floor, on his back, legs tangled in a broken chair, head propped up with a pile of papers in the dim kitchen. Albert looked up at the ceiling and saw where a fixture had pulled loose, and then at the coil of rope lying with the shattered lamp on the table. He looked more closely at the rope. "You all right?" he asked.

The old man's eyes fixed on the case of beer in Albert's arms. He said, from the floor, repeating the first few words as he caught his breath, "My name is Harold McCracken, Harold McCracken, poet and drunk. Your neighbour, I believe."

Albert had been released the first week of April, same day as Jerome, but his probation order included a prohibition to associate with known addicts or felons, and so far he had obeyed, though he had been drinking beer in the days between appointments with Sam, Samantha, his PO, despite the same prohibition for alcohol, drugs, and firearms. His mother had refused to take him back in, telling him she would lend him first and last, let him take all her old pots and pans, but he had to get a job and stay clean for at least six months before she wanted to see him again. He found an inexpensive apartment, a walk-up on James

44

North, above the Italian coffee place and the Portuguese Travel shop, foregoing one or two rentals he thought could lead to suicide within a few weeks.

Through a temp agency he had been sent out on a roofing job with a crew of Newfies, which kept him busy, paid for the rent and beer, and led to a series of jobs cleaning and repairing gutters, roofs, eaves. He was outside most of the day, up and down ladders and scaffolds, his jeans and hands scraped and raw from asphalt shingles, but getting healthier and stronger. Most days he was picked up by a couple of guys in a King Cab, one of them already toking, then up a ladder, hauling shingles, the guys talking about sex, always sex, anything reminding them of sex, the event, the action, the meaning, the method. He turned down the offer of a joint, knowing he was already pushing it with the beer, but, c'mon, after a day in the sun, the wind....His fingers grew raw then callused from handling the shingles, his skin grew darker, stripping old roofs, tacking on new twenty year shingles, crawling around on the roof, these losers he worked with smoking joints all day, telling their stories. But, the end of the day, aching, sometimes neck and shoulders wind burned, dirty and spent, sprawled in his one good chair, a cold Molson in hand, he felt good. He knew he would sleep well, until the alarm woke him at six. Only his days off, one or two a week, or the occasional rainy day when the only work available was outdoors, did his demons of discontent appear: boredom, restlessness, yearning, anxiety. One of the guys on the job sold him a big screen plasma TV and a DVD player, of suspicious origins, but cheap enough. He could call up an old friend, like Kyle, or

45

hang in a bar, but he reached for the remote instead and watched all the movies he had missed during his five months away.

The walls were thin. He could often hear arguing, a toilet flushing, television from several doors down the corridor, but little from his next door neighbour. He kept to himself, slipping in and out with hardly a glance down the hall.

On this day in early May, back from a day of roofing, hot and dirty, carrying a case of beer under one arm and a bucket of Kentucky Fried under the other, Albert was trying to manoeuvre his key into the door without putting down either when a loud crash and a stream of profanity stopped him. It was coming from next door, his neighbour, an old guy who had appeared a couple of weeks after Albert had moved in. Albert hesitated, noticed his neighbour's door was slightly ajar. He put his key back in his pocket and walked the few steps to the next apartment door, still carrying his beer and chicken, calling out, "You all right in there?"

When the answer was a second crashing sound Albert pushed the door open with his foot. He stepped inside the musty apartment and found the small corridor filled, but for a small passage, with piles of newspapers, magazines and books. In a room on his immediate left the piles continued on tables, chairs, on the floor. Edging sideways with the case of beer under one arm, the bucket of chicken under the other, Albert continued along the tight passage to a darkened room. He could make out a sink, a refrigerator, stove, and then the table, and then Harry lying on the floor.

Albert found a clear corner of the kitchen table for the case of beer and bucket of chicken. "Anything broken...I mean besides the chair?"

Harry shook his head, moved his legs and said, "Only my pride and my faith in mankind."

Albert reached down and helped him to his feet. And as if there was nothing unusual in these circumstances, while brushing himself off, ignoring the shambles, Harry said, "Perhaps we should retire to your abode for our repast. I doubt I have two clean plates."

Albert looked at the man, maybe in his sixties, a little shorter than himself, grey hair, full beard, an ill-fitting brown suit over a blue shirt. He said, "Harold..."

The old man interrupted him, said, "Harry. Just plain Harry to neighbours and friends, lovers and others." He picked up the bucket of chicken, left the kitchen and entered the passageway to his door, leaving Albert with no choice but to follow with the beer.

In his own kitchen, while Harry sat, Albert found a couple of plates and opened the case of beer. They had consumed four beer and a few pieces of chicken in silence before Albert looked over at Harry, saw him eating with good appetite, and said, "You wanna die, there's gotta be easier ways, Harry."

Harry paused in his eating for a moment and replied, "Now that's where you're wrong, my young friend. There are no easy ways. Just fast ways and slow ways."

The beer was hitting Albert. Only two, going on three, but he'd been out in the sun all day and hadn't eaten since noon. He took a long swallow and said, "Well, it's the fast way for me, man. Time comes, I wanna go out quick. Bang." He mimed one finger at his temple.

Harry said, "We don't always get choices, Albert." He pulled another piece of chicken from the bucket.

All day long with the Newfie roofers they'd been talking about sex, every object, every action reminding one of them of doing it, in every possible way, in every possible combination. Mostly lies, Albert assumed. This, at least, was a different topic, and Albert was feeling suddenly garrulous. He said, "Shit, I figure you get the cancer you just put a forty-five to your head and pow. It's all she wrote." He mimed the action again, this time with two fingers. But as he did this, he felt the veil of alcohol lifting, revealing a place his mouth was taking him against his will.

Harry said, between mouthfuls, "Either way, it is not easy. It is not an easy thing."

Albert said, "The fuck it isn't. You were just in there doing it, for Christ's sakes. Now you're eating my chicken and drinking my beer."

Harry said, "It is your beer and I am your guest. We can talk of something else."

Albert took another swallow. "Right."

But Harry, always alert to fragile defences and the truth beneath, said, "We all die, my friend, some fast, some slow, some young, some old, some by their own hand. But it is never an easy thing."

"Fuck it isn't," said Albert, reaching for another beer.

48

Harry looked at him. "Have you tried?" he asked.

"No," said Albert. "I haven't tried."

"So you don't know yet, do you? And you're of an age when death is still, for you, a proposition, a theory."

"It's no fucking theory for me, man. It's not just theory." He recognized this was getting away from himself, that something was rising in his throat, but he continued. "And you were trying to hang yourself a little while ago and now you're sitting here eating chicken. Like there was nothing fucking to it. Here today, gone tomorrow. Who gives a shit anyway?" Albert rummaged in the paper bag from the bucket of chicken. He found a packet of ketchup, tore it open and squeezed it onto his plate. Harry watched him without responding. Albert heard himself go on, heard himself saying it. "All you need's a fucking loaded gun and a bottle of whiskey, man, that's all. That'll do it."

Harry said, "You know someone who did just that, don't you?"

Albert said, "Let's change the subject. Subject's closed. You fell off a chair. I bin out in the sun all day. I should have picked up twenty-four. Lakeport. Buck a bottle."

Harry said, "Who do you know killed himself?"

"Shit, man. Did I say that? Did I say I knew someone killed himself? Did I say that? I don't remember saying that."

Harry said, "You know someone. Someone close, I think."

Albert put his beer down, leaned forward. "What makes you think I know someone? Shit. You don't know dick. You don't know dick about me."

Harry looked away. "Forget it then. I shouldn't meddle."

Albert got up, pulled his chair back. He looked in his empty refrigerator. He took one of the few remaining bottles of beer from the carton. He sat back in his chair away from the table. He had opened a door. He couldn't stop himself. He took a long swallow. He said, "You think I knew him? You think I fucking knew him? I didn't know him. I didn't have a fucking clue.... It was the old man, that's fucking who. My father. You satisfied now?"

Harry didn't speak; Albert went back to the refrigerator, looked inside again, found no escape. He sat back down. "He drank a bottle of Canadian Club, and did it right there in his La Z Boy. I knew him, huh? I didn't know nothing. He just bought the goddamn thing from Parks a month before. You believe that? A fucking leather chair."

Harry said, "I'm sorry, Albert. I wouldn't have asked about it if I'd known."

But Albert was deep inside himself now, talking, seeing it happen. "You ever seen the mess that makes? You ever seen it? We had to throw the goddamn thing out. A three hundred dollar chair. Took it to the dump, and the bastards charged us to dump it. Ten bucks. The thing's covered with blood and brain cells and the bastards charge us ten bucks to dump it." The thought hung in the air. Albert was silent for a minute. Harry sat with his head bowed as if in prayer. Albert went on, "That night, right? Eight, nine o'clock I come home, I bin hanging out somewhere, doing a little weed with my buddy Kyle, I come home and he's in the basement cleaning his rifle. Cleaning his fucking rifle. It's not hunting season and he's cleaning his rifle. Nowhere near hunting

50

season. And I do fuck all, is what I do. I look in on him, sure, but then go off upstairs, put the earphones on and crank up the stereo, smoke some more. He's in the basement sitting there cleaning his rifle, fucking hours he's cleaning his rifle."

Harry looked up, said, "There's nothing you can do if somebody wants to end it, there's nothing you can do."

Albert: "That's bullshit, Harry. Bullshit. How long's it take to clean a fucking rifle? He's just waiting to be asked. She's upstairs corked on Valium or some shit, or maybe just too scared to do anything, I got the headphones on, smoking a doob, waiting for a call to get me outa there, and he's sitting in the basement cleaning away."

Harry leaned back in his chair, listening.

Albert continued, "Nobody calls. I fall asleep. Then around midnight he loads the rifle, takes it upstairs, sits in his new La Z Boy.....You ever hear a rifle go off inside a house?... That moment... That moment I knew. I was asleep and it woke me up and I knew. And I knew that I'd known for two fucking days he was gonna do it. Two fucking days....He was a fucking loser, you know that, a fucking loser. Everything he tried turned to shit. Everything..."

"I'm sorry, son." Said Harry, aware of the word he had used.

"Yeah," said Albert, pulling himself out of his story. "So don't fucking hang yourself while I'm living next door. I don't need it. I just don't fucking need it."

They finished the chicken and drank the rest of the beer in silence. Albert cleaned off the table, sat back down. Only the kitchen light on, above the table, the rest in darkness. The refrigerator humming on, then off. Albert said, "I've still got the suicide note. Said he would have done it earlier but waited until I finished grade 12. Didn't want his death to upset my schooling. Funny thing was, I hadn't been going to school regular for a couple of years. Dropped out way before. He had to know that."

"Maybe it was sarcasm," ventured Harry. "Though I don't think it's a sentiment common to suicide notes."

"Naw," said Albert. "He just never got anything right."

7

All the lousy little poets coming round

Beverlee was saying, "They got in a fight, that's all. And he wasn't even in it to begin with. He tried to break it up. And he's the one got arrested when the cops came."

Sam was listening to this woman, on a supervision order for her eight year old who had witnessed what the Children's Aid called 'Domestic Violence'. Her ex-boyfriend Mike now on probation and not allowed to go within a hundred meters of the house.

Sam said, "You want the probation order changed so Mike can visit but you're now living with Mike's friend Shawn, one of the other guys in the fight? That about it?"

"Yeah, but it wasn't Shawn's fault either. He was ready to leave but Alvin didn't wanna go."

Sam said, "So we got Alvin, Shawn, and Mike, at your house that night?"

"And Joe."

"So we've got Mike and three other guys at the house?"

"I invited them over, just to talk, you know, socialize."

"It's subsidized housing, right? North end?"

"Uhhuh. I don't see what that's got to do with it."

"Nothing. Just trying to picture the scene, that's all."

"It's a three bedroom, on account of Kimberley."

"Kimberley?"

"She's thirteen. Staying with her grandmother for now."

"Allissa's eight, Kimberley thirteen. Have I got it right?"

"Right. But not the same father."

"Mike's not the father of either one?"

"No. But he's good with Allissa. Allissa really likes him."

"Kimberley doesn't?"

"She's thirteen, what can I tell you?"

"Okay. So it's Saturday night. You're living with Mike and Allissa, or at least Mike's been living in your house for some time. You invite three other guys over to party?"

"He's not living at my house."

"He's there most nights? His clothes in a closet? His toothbrush in the bathroom?"

"Yeah, but...."

"It's okay, Beverlee. That's just between you and social services. Nothing to do with me."

"Okay. Mike was living with us, three, maybe four years."

"And you invite three other guys over to party that Saturday night?"

"Just to talk, listen to music. They're my friends. There's nothing wrong with that."

"And they get in a fight."

"That was later."

"So what time did they get in a fight?"

"About ten."

"That's pretty early."

"Ten in the morning."

"Ahh. So you have an all night drinking party and a fight breaks out the next morning."

"I didn't want them to drive that night, after they'd been drinking. Why are you sitting there judging me? I've got a right to socialize, just like anybody else."

"I'm not judging you. I'm just trying to get the story straight."

"Well, the fight was stupid. Shawn wanted to leave. Alvin kept saying not yet. He wasn't ready to leave. Shawn got into a shoving match with Alvin and Mike tried to break it up. Then the cops came and arrested Mike. And Joe was the worst but they didn't arrest him. It's all such bullshit."

"Why didn't Alvin want to leave?"

"How the hell should I know? What difference does it make?"

"Okay, so who called the cops?"

"Somebody. A neighbour. I think when the front window got broken. You get a lot of nosy neighbours in Housing. Stick their noses into everything. He's the one the cops should have taken away. I'm pretty sure he's dealing."

Sam had closed the door to her office when Beverlee came in to plead her case for Mike, but through the narrow glass panel next to the door she could see a pair of legs and work boots in the waiting room. She checked her watch, decided the legs probably belonged to Albert Wesnicki, and that he could sit there and wait until she got this Beverlee/Mike thing straight. Beverlee, spelled with two e's, mother of Allissa spelled with two l's, didn't see why she needed a supervision

55

order for her kid and why Mike couldn't visit Allissa any time he wanted. Mike had been Sam's client on probation for possession for six months, and now Children's Aid had gone to court to add a restraining order limiting him to 100 meters of the house. Beverlee had told her she was 28, full time mother to eight year-old Allissa, and had been full time mother to Kimberley before she decided she liked her grandmother's house rules better. Living on mothers' allowance, doing her best, though no longer speaking with her own mother on account of Kimberley.

Sam asked, "Not allowing Mike anywhere near the house is pretty severe. Was there anything else happened besides the fight?"

"Kimberley may have said some things that got Children's Aid in a knot. You know how things are. Thirteen year-olds lie, all the time."

Sam said, "Okay, but what I really don't understand, if you're now living with Shawn, why you'd want Mike to visit in the first place."

"Because Mike is Allissa's father, well, not her real father, but as good as a father, and they have a whatdayacallit, a bond."

Sam was only a few years older than Beverlee, and she hadn't been around as much, but she did know one thing. When a woman wants her ex to visit, it's probably about money. "Mike still have his job?"

"Yeah, of course. He only spent one night in jail. He's still working."

"And how does he feel with Shawn sharing your bed?"

"He's cool with that. It was over between us a long time anyway."

"So you and Shawn had a thing going before this fight?"

"That's none of your business. You're sitting there judging me. I didn't get raised the same way you did. I was out of the house at fifteen. I wasn't allowed to raise my first baby. I only got Kimberley back when she was nine, and now she's gone again. You got no right to judge me. You don't even have any children of your own. You don't know how hard it is."

Beverlee was a little plump, otherwise not bad looking, if you ignored the tongue ring and the spider-web tattoo that peaked above her collar on the left side of her neck, and the shock of crimson in her dark hair, that would have been cute on a teen, but it was all down hill from here, Sam was thinking, unkindly. She'd been trading on cute into her late twenties, and time was running out. Two kids, the oldest already skipping school, smoking marijuana, shoplifting. Sam could picture her. They all looked the same that age, tight low jeans, little belly showing, metal in her ears, tongue, and nose, some weird colour in her hair, attitude on her lips, knew too much about some things and too little about others, pregnant before she turns sixteen. And then there was the eight year old, Allissa. Sam imagined her still sweet, already exposed to far more than she should be, but only precocious now, in trouble later. Sam tried her best to detach herself, stay professional, but, here she was, older than Beverlee, no children of her own, no prospects, had put herself through university, supported herself, dutifully or fearfully staying on the pill throughout, not sure she'd

57

make a great mother herself, but she sure as hell would do a better job than Beverlee with two e's.

She said, "Look, it's a court order. Mike is not allowed to visit. I'd have to go back to court to convince a judge on your behalf that the order should be lifted. For them to even listen to me there'd have to be a good reason. I haven't heard a real good reason yet."

"What about Allissa? Don't her feelings count for anything?"

"Beverlee, my sweet, you are damned lucky CAS didn't scoop her up, put her in a foster home."

"Allissa didn't even see the fight. She wasn't even up yet. She was sleeping in. I'm a good mother to her."

"The report says she was there."

"That was after. The cops arrive, sirens and everything. That's what woke her up. She didn't know what was going on."

"She was sleeping in because?"

'Well, she got to bed a little late that night. That's all right on the weekends. We were playing music. She kept coming down to see what was going on. I kept sending her back to bed."

Sam paused for a minute. She let the scene play in her mind a little. She couldn't imagine it was just booze, but this Beverlee was not her probie, just her probie's ex-girlfriend. Four guys drinking and snorting or smoking or something, music loud, Beverlee flirting with at least two of them, keeping the tension high, poor little Allissa trying to sleep upstairs.

She said, "Well, have you at least learned anything from this?"

"Like what would I learn?"

"Like maybe if you have an eight year old kid in the house it's not a good idea to have an all night drinking party with your current boyfriend, your future boyfriend and two other guys."

"See, you're judging me. You're sitting there judging me. You've got no right to do that. I think I'll leave now." Shifting a little but not really getting up.

Sam said, "You know, I said I wasn't judging you before. I lied. I am judging you. It's my job. Of course I'm judging you."

"Well you don't know nothing about my life. It's not like I had decent parents who taught me this stuff. It's not my fault Mike got in a fight."

"Beverlee, I'm real forgiving about the stupid things people do. Like having a party that gets out of hand. It's the bullshit I have trouble with."

"I'm not bullshitting. I'm telling you the truth."

"Look, here's the truth. It's Saturday night. You've been doing it with two guys, one at home, one out of the home. You're bored. You put the kid to bed and call up the other guy to come over. You call a couple more guys because you don't wanna be obvious. It's gonna be an all night drinking party and you're gonna have two if not four guys wanting to take you to bed. They get in a fight and you try to make out like it's a surprise, an accidental thing. Now…hold on a minute….I'll bet Mike is saying he's not paying child support if he doesn't get to see the kid. So you want him to be able to see Allissa. Take her out to McDonalds or something. It's really about the money."

59

"It's not about the money. You people are just so judgemental. He's like her father. I don't believe in coming between a kid and her father."

Sam got up from the office chair and moved behind her desk. Tapping on the keyboard she said, "You lead a very complicated life, Beverlee."

Beverlee said, "I can handle it."

"I'm seeing your Mike four thirty tomorrow. If he shows I'll see what I can do."

"He'll show. Why wouldn't he show?"

"I'll do what I can, see if I can convince him to pay support for Allissa."

"That's it then."

"That's it."

"Don't tell him I was here, please."

Sam watched Beverlee with two e's leave. She found herself irritated with this woman but wasn't sure why. She stepped from her office, walked across the waiting room to a corridor that led to the washrooms, on the way telling Albert she would just be a few minutes. Albert glanced up at her, said, "No problem."

In the mirror above the small sink she looked at the reflection of her eyes. Flecks of green on light brown, no makeup, frown lines showing, dirty blonde hair shorter than usual, in the latest bob thanks to Giselle, which would look okay if she put a little colour on her lips, accented the eyes. She liked to think this Beverlee's looks would be gone in a few years. Then she'd have to provide both the booze and a few lines of Coke to get the boys over. A little grin played on her lips as she recognized her own spitefulness, as if she were back in High School, competing for these guys. But here she is going on 32 herself, twice a week hooking up with a married cop, no children of her own. Her mother would be calling tonight and once again she'd have to come up with a story why she wasn't dating someone she could bring to supper. Her mother had actually come out with it once, asked directly, "You're not lesbian, are you, dear?" And then she had hastily added, "Not that there's anything wrong with that." And they had both laughed, her mother's laugh a little tentative.

On the way back to her office she signalled Albert, with a slight tilt of her head, to follow her. She was thinking some of the guys she saw, it would be easier if she were clearly, unmistakably lesbian. Albert was not bad looking, more intelligence in his eyes than most of her clients, a nice tan and a few muscles from his job, unruly hair gelled with blonde tips. He'd clean up quite nicely.

She closed her office door and sat behind her desk. He took one of the chairs on the other side. With guys like Albert you had to establish the rules of their relationship from the very beginning.

She said, "You going to test negative today, Albert?"

"Yeah. Of course."

"So what's got you so antsy?"

'Nothing. I'm cool. Maybe I didn't sleep so well last night, that's all. It's a shit part of town, sirens, guys coming out of bars all hours."

"I hear it's an up and coming neighbourhood. Little galleries, restaurants."

"All those men's clubs, you know, guys hanging out avoiding their wives. I believe a lot of cocaine exchanges hands in the back rooms."

"You're telling me this because?"

"Nothing. I mean, this is Hamilton. You gotta be realistic."

"You're staying away from it?"

"Absolutely."

"And attending your NA meetings?"

"Couple of times a week. But I wanted to tell you about that. I'm working every day. Don't get home until seven most nights. The last thing I need is going out, drinking coffee, listening to these guys tell their war stories, some of them still using."

"It's in your probation order."

"Yeah, but if I stay clean, can I get by with once a week, maybe once every second week?"

"Albert, you stay clean, when I ask you if you're attending NA, just say 'yes' and I'll leave it at that."

"Okay. That's a deal."

"You look like you've been in the sun a lot. Are you getting steady work?"

"Every day it doesn't rain."

"And after the construction, roofing season, you have any thoughts?"

"Like the book says, one day at a time."

"Planning a little is good sometimes."

"Yeah, well, I'll still be on probation. Can't travel far."

"Albert, you know, you've actually got a brain. You could go back to school. Get your grade 12 in a couple of months, go on to College. Get it all paid for."

"I hated school."

"You were a teenager then. Maybe it'd be different now."

"You think? Maybe."

"The pamphlets are in the waiting room. You can do correspondence or attend one of the adult learning centres."

"I'll think about it."

Samantha shifted in her chair. Getting these guys to think past the next sunset was hard. When they're hustling, it's all within these particular twenty-four hours. Tomorrow'll take care of itself. Money, a debt, a job, a score, getting high. As long as these twenty-four hours are in the bag they don't worry about the next. Never-ending adolescence. She sighed, leaned forward, changed the topic. "How's your mother?"

"She doesn't want to see me till I've had six months clean. I don't blame her. "

"Not seeing her at all?"

"I phone about once a week. We talk a bit. But she's holding tough on that six month deal. When I was in jail she'd send these postcards once a week, just said on them, 'Wish you were here.' Signed, 'Your mother.'"

"I think I like your mother."

"Yeah. She's got a sense of humour. Despite everything."

"So you've got several reasons to stay clean and make a life for yourself."

Albert didn't say anything. She had started him thinking about the fall, when construction and roofing would slow down. What the hell would he do with himself?

Sam held his eyes for a moment, then she reached for some papers on her desk and said, "Okay, Albert Wesnicki. Same time, same place two weeks from now. Grab a cup and piss in it on your way out."

"You ain't gonna watch me?"

She didn't answer. He didn't stand.

"Something else on your mind?"

"I was just gonna tell you. There's an old guy lives in the apartment next door. Tried to hang himself last week."

"And?"

"Nothing really. I found him. He's okay now."

"What are you trying to tell me, Albert?"

"I dunno. Just wanted to tell you about it."

"I remember your father killed himself, didn't he?"

"Yeah. But that was years ago. That wasn't the thing."

"No? You telling me there's no connection?"

"Forget it. I'll see you in two weeks."

"You don't want to talk about it?"

"Naw. Not today."

"Okay. Two weeks it is. Don't forget the specimen on your way out."

8

I've seen the future, brother

Jerome said, "Look, this'll be easy. No problem. I got it all figured."

Albert had been looking around the room. He shook his head. "Last easy one cost me five months."

Jerome said, "Shit. You weren't paying attention is all. You were paying attention you could have stepped away from it. And from what you told me in the joint you took a swing at a cop. Didn't have to go down that way at all."

It had been a hot dry summer, the temperature sometimes hitting the mid thirties, and over forty with humidity factored in. Work had been steady with a building and renovation boom in the suburbs, the Newfies proving to be hard workers, even the one stoned most of the day. When they got off the topic of sex they talked about the Rock, their families, their buddies, the weather back home, the all night parties, working on the lobster boats. Some of the other labourers they used for bigger jobs wanted their pay in cash, up front, and seldom showed the next day. Albert was reliable and so they gave him steady work.

Out in the sun, getting healthy, surrounded by the kidding, self-deprecating, boasting, taunting, scatological rituals of man talk, the tat-tat-tat of pressure hammers and staple guns, Albert felt thankful and safe. He bought a small air conditioner from the same guy who sold him the Plasma TV, installed it in his living room window above James Street. On the first stifling evening in early July, Harry invited himself in, to sit in the chilled and drier air until his own apartment had cooled enough for, as he would call it, human habitation.

They didn't speak again about Albert's father or Harry's suicide attempt, if that's what it was. Albert mostly listened, or watched cable TV, while Harry sipped from a red plastic juice glass and told stories. Harry's preoccupation with himself, his own history, his writing, (as if anybody cared about poetry these days), could be annoying, but Albert knew his old friends and the streets and bars and clubs were not safe, especially with money in his pocket. He stayed with beer while Harry drank from his cup. Harry had arrived with shaking hands and empty cup a couple of times, and had then drunk Albert's beer, until Albert purchased a bottle he kept in the back cupboard for just such occasions.

He talked to his mother a few times. She had told him she was happy for him and maybe by Thanksgiving or Christmas she would be ready to have him in her house again. He saw Sam every two weeks, a quick check in and out, and made sure he drank no beer the night before.

Small galleries were popping up on James that summer, in storefronts neighbouring the Portuguese restaurants, Chinese groceries, Cafes and Clubs. Albert shopped on James, getting his work shirts from Morgensterns, fish from the Atlantic Fish Market, meat from a butcher around the corner. Knots of Italian and Portuguese men talked and smoked on the sidewalks, tall Sudanese refugees floated by, Chinese haggled over prices. There was always an addict or alcoholic in the mix, going on by, moving from the Mission to the Mall or the square by Ferguson, but at night they grew in number, slipping in and out of the café once owned, maybe still owned indirectly, by the Mob. A few times Albert thought he recognized a face from the jail but would quickly avert his eyes, and hurry on by. One of them he knew as Bill or Billy, usually in pretty rough shape, scars and bruises on his hands and face, walking up James with determination, the look on his face showing his mind working on a private grievance.

Albert kept to himself, remained a stranger in his own city, determined to stay away from drugs, do his time, just get by until…. That was the question. Until what? A day at a time, they said, at his NA meetings. Take a day at a time. One evening Harry had told him that life is what happens to you while you're trying to figure out what to do with your life. He'd waited for a smile from Albert and then gone on to say that he'd known a few men and women who actually planned their lives, scripted them, and followed the script. But where was the fun in that? The real problem, he said, is how one can ever know his plan is right. We can't know what the universe has in store for us, Harry said, looking a little grim as he tipped his plastic cup to his lips. Albert's probation officer was cut from more practical cloth. She broached the subject on every visit. But thinking of the future only reminded Albert of the hole he was in, the one, his mother would point out to him when he phoned, that he had dug himself. Just taking care of day-to-day shit, living sober and staying out of trouble, was work enough he decided, and occasionally, just occasionally, he found himself noticing the movement of leaves in the trees, the warmth of the sun on his shoulders, the squirrels chasing one another across a fragile branch, the rich and abundant life around him.

The work slowed in October, and then a week of rain left him unemployed, and he began to worry about the future.

On the fourth rainy day they hadn't called him to work he went out to see where his father was buried. He didn't know why. He stood under a tree in the drizzle, looking over the headstones. He thought he would feel anger, but instead a wave of sadness passed through him, and loneliness. And then futility.

It was on his way back to his apartment that he ran into Jerome. Collar pulled up around his neck he kept moving, acknowledging Jerome with a shrug and a mumbled, "Yeah."

But Jerome caught up with him, stepped in front of him, said, "Albert. Albert, my man. You're fucking soaked. Lemme buy you a drink, get you out of the rain."

He was wet, chilled. His apartment offered little on a slow dreary day and they were only a block from the Regal. He said, "Why the fuck not." Though he knew why not.

As they walked, Jerome said, "Where you been hangin' man? Haven't seen ya since you got out. Getting lots of pussy? Uh?"

Albert said, "I've been working. Roofing. Construction."

"You didn't answer my question."

"What question?"

"What question. The only question, my son. Well, one of three anyway. In no particular order of importance. Got any money? Made your peace with God? Getting any pussy?"

"I had no idea you were a spiritual man."

"Still avoiding the question."

"Okay," said Albert. "My share. I'm getting my share."

"Yeah? Bullshit." Said Jerome, as he led Albert through the door into the Regal and took a table across from the bar in the back room.

Albert took a side trip to the washroom where he shed his jacket, shook off the water, mopped at his hair with a paper towel. When he returned there was beer on the table. He sat and stared at it, considering. Not that he hadn't been drinking beer contrary to his probation order, but he'd been doing it in private, only Harry as a witness. Now he was breaching three lines in his order: associating with a known felon, in a bar, drinking.

Jerome took a long swallow from his glass, leaned back in his chair, looked around the bar. He said, as if it had just popped into his mind, "I got a thing going."

When Albert didn't respond Jerome leaned forward, said, "What have you got going? Nothing. I can see it."

"I got plans," said Albert.

"Yeah? Tell your old buddy."

"Nah. You're right. Nothing special happening."

"So, you want in on something. Easy ten grand, know what I'm saying?"

'No such thing," said Albert, looking around at the few customers hiding from the afternoon.

"This one is. Like taking candy from a baby. I got it all figured."

Albert looked directly at Jerome. He shook his head. "Last easy one cost me five months."

Jerome said, "Shit. You weren't paying attention is all. You were paying attention you could have stepped away from it. And from what you told me in the joint you took a swing at a cop. Didn't have to go down that way at all."

When Albert said nothing, Jerome went on, "Look, I'm basically an honest guy, right?"

Albert gave him that mouth-twisted raised eyebrow look that means 'You're shitting me.'

"Don't give me that look, man."

"What? I didn't say nothing."

"You didn't have to say nothing. That look you gave me. Said it right there. Said you think I'm fulla shit."

"You gotta admit…"

"What? What I gotta admit?"

"You've been convicted of stuff."

"Yeah, so?"

"So, like officially, you know, officially, on the record, proven in a court of law, you're not an honest guy."

"That's fucking different. You should know that. I don't lie to my friends. Which is where it's at. The bank, the cops, women, fucking lawyers, okay. That's a different story. But not to my friends. I'm honest with my friends."

"Alls I'm saying is that officially you're not an honest guy."

"What the fuck does officially have to do with anything? I mean what the fuck?"

"Okay."

"So what's with okay?

"Nothing. Forget it. Doesn't mean nothing. You're basically an honest guy."

"Fucking right. Can't stand bullshitters. Never could."

Albert's glass remained untouched. He'd been staring into it like a man who didn't understand what to do with the amber liquid in his glass. Like he was from fucking Mars, Jerome was thinking. Jerome said, "You gonna drink that or build a shrine? Cause if you don't drink it soon, Wally'll be over joining us."

Albert looked over at the guy with the messy beard in the corner. He was watching them, or more specifically, he was eyeballing the full, untouched glass of beer on their table. "You know him?" Albert looked back at Jerome.

"Forget him, "said Jerome. "Told me one time he wears a sheet of Aluminum foil in his shorts. You believe that? I wasn't asking him. Just happened to take a piss at the same time. He turns to me and says this thing about the foil in his drawers. To protect his gentiles he tells me. Gentiles. That's what he said. Swear to God."

"Is he circumcised?" Asked Albert.

"What the fuck has that got to do with anything? You think I took a look?"

"Gentiles. That was all. It was just a thought."

71

"You think too much, you know that. That is your problem. Look. You're thinking about drinking that beer. You're fucking driving everybody nuts thinking. In the end you'll fucking drink it. You always do. You just drive yourself nuts making decisions, when the decision's already made. Made long ago for Christ's sakes. Take this thing I'm gonna tell you about. You'll think and think and weigh up every angle, but in the end, you'll do it. It's in your nature, man. You gotta learn to give in to your nature."

Jerome is thin and tall, and he's got these shoulders that belong to another guy. Like there should be a lot more beef on him but it's been burned off. He walks like he's carrying a heavy bag in each hand. He's got tattoos up both arms, something on his neck as well, and this slick black hair with sideburns.

Jerome's on a roll now and Albert knows all he can do is listen. "Look. This is what you're doing. Tell me if I got it wrong. You're thinking about the last few times they did a random urine. Right? And whether or not tonight would be a night the bastards pick. Tonight's the night they call you and order you in. You're calculating the fucking odds. You're looking for an edge. You know what I think. I think guys like you and me we got no edge. We're in the program. So drink the fucking beer. A, because you will eventually, and B, because you gonna get screened you gonna get screened. They wanna bust you they gonna bust you. All there is to it. The only thing we got going for us is they don't wanna work too hard. They're not going to put you back in for one lousy beer."

Albert's not really thinking about the beer. He's looking at it but not thinking about it. He's thinking about where Jerome is going with this. What's this thing he's got in mind? He'll wait for it. He may drink the fucking beer he may not. But Jerome has one thing right. He's in the program. Or he was in the program, until this past summer when he'd managed to stay clean, earn a bit of money. But the roofing jobs were drying up as the weather turned, a cold poor winter ahead.

Jerome was saying, "So when I tell you something, man, you can bank on it. So I tell you this thing is a sure thing, you know you're getting it straight."

Albert decided he would drink the beer, but not until Jerome tells him what this thing is. The full glass just sitting there was really irritating Jerome. A bug up his ass.

Jerome was waving off the server, the one with the hard body and good tits but a face looked like an old mail sack. "He hasn't started the first one, for Christ's sakes," Jerome said.

"This thing you got," said Albert.

"All right. Christ. You wanna hear it? You wanna hear it now? You doing me a favour by listening? All right. I'll tell ya. There's a house over on Wentworth. Black guy from Toronto. Sets himself up there dealing."

"Yeah?"

"He's not connected. He's freelance. Won't last long, but right now he's holding maybe ten, twenty G's.

"Gotta be more to this story."

"He's got no protection."

"And you know this…"

"Arlene. She was balling the guy for a while. She wants thirty percent."

"I'm still listening."

Jerome wasn't looking at Albert. He was staring at the full glass of beer. "Okay. Here's the deal. Arlene's inside. She opens the door for us. Nothing to it."

"Thought you said she was balling the guy."

"She's still buying from him. May not be balling him. But she still has her needs, man."

"Why is she turning on the guy?"

"How the fuck do I know? You telling me you understand women? Maybe he's hitting her. Maybe he can't get it up. Maybe she likes me. It don't matter why, long as she's doing it. You got women figured out, you let me know."

Albert could picture the whole thing. They'd wait in some dive over near Wentworth till long past midnight. Drink a few while they're waiting. Jerome would pop some Crystal Meth to get up for it. Maybe he'd pick the right house, maybe he wouldn't. Arlene would forget to unlock the front door. Maybe she'd sell them out. Once they get in, they find the black guy's got a couple of friends over. One of them is packing. Or Jerome's carrying himself. "No guns man, no violence. In and out," he'd say. But Jerome wouldn't get into this without a little backup. He'll be packing too.

74

Albert figured there was a lot to consider here. Lots of possible outcomes, besides Jerome's idea of a good time. Something goes wrong. Something always goes wrong.

But Wally was getting up out of his chair now. Holding onto the back of the next chair until he finds his legs. His eyes on the glass of beer, now one foot out like he was making sure the floor was solid before putting any weight on it, feeling with his toes. You could see the edge of foil riding up over his belt. That's when Albert's right hand closed around the full glass of beer and lifted it off the table, kind of played with it a bit, and then swallowed some down. It wasn't cold anymore, but when that first mouthful washed down Albert's throat, it felt like he was coming home.

9

It is murder

Jerome had a buzz on. Albert was cool. He'd had a couple of beer to steady himself, that was all. The neighbourhood was quiet. You could just hear the odd truck on Main, a couple of blocks down Wentworth. They'd gotten to the back yard of the house, feeling for steps to the porch. This house was one of an old row of two and a half story brick homes, maybe 90 years old, many cut up into apartments, each with small fenced back yard. It was dark as piss.

"It's dark as piss," Jerome said.

"She couldn't very well leave the porch light on," said Albert. But he was beginning to feel wrong. They'd found the house all right, and slipped down the side to the back. They could make out a porch and a back door off the porch but there seemed to be no steps up to the porch. Jerome was about to pull himself up by a post. "Fucking things rotten. Careful you don't go through."

Jerome pulled himself up. The post held. He stepped over to the door. He said, "C'mon." He groped for the handle as Albert pulled himself up. "Place is a mess," said Jerome. "They should complain to the landlord."

Jerome had found the handle now and Albert took a deep breath as Jerome twisted it and pushed. Nothing. He twisted and pushed again. Nothing again. "Fuck. It's still locked. That stupid cunt."

"She didn't mean the front door, did she?" Albert said.

"No."

"Or a side door? Did you see a side door?"

"I wasn't looking for a side door. She said back door, I'm pretty sure."

"What else are you pretty sure about?"

"What the fuck's wrong with you?"

"Are you pretty sure she's in there? Are you pretty sure the guy's got twenty grand? Are you pretty sure he's got no help?"

"Fuck you." Said Jerome. And Albert knew instantly he shouldn't have mocked him, because Jerome took a step back, raised his leg and kicked the door in. The door cracked open with a crunching slam that reverberated through the neighbourhood. Some dogs answered back.

"Christ almighty," said Albert.

"Told you the fucking door'd be open," said Jerome. He stepped over the shattered door into the kitchen. Albert followed. His brain told him to leave and cut his losses but his feet followed Jerome. There was noise above them, voices, then feet running.

Jerome felt for a light switch as the feet came down the stairs fast, moving away from the kitchen, toward the front, and then on the landing, and then down the hallway toward them. Albert backed into something in the dark. His eyes were accommodating. The footsteps stopped and a shadowed figure loomed in the doorway to the kitchen. Jerome hadn't found the light, which gave them a small advantage.

With his feet, Albert felt for the edge of the broken door to the back porch.

The silhouetted figure said, "What the fuck. Who the fuck you think…..."

And Jerome shot him. The sudden blast startled Albert. He tripped on the broken door and fell to his knees. Again the neighbourhood dogs howled. The silhouette fell back into the hall, saying, simply, "Fuck. You shot me. You fucking shot me."

"Jesus, Jesus, Jesus." Said Albert. "What the fuck you do that for?'

"I had no choice, man. He gave me no choice."

"Like fuck you had no choice. Where'd the gun come from?"

"You with me or not?" Said Jerome. "Cause if you want out now, just go. I don't give a shit."

"He's still alive," said Albert. The crumpled figure was moaning and coughing.

"He'll bleed out. Let's take a look upstairs."

Albert knew this was his problem. He could have said no at the Regal, when Jerome told him about the thing. He could have pulled out when they found the back door locked. He could have run when the guy came down the hall. But he was into this now, like he had to see it through, had to see how it comes out.

Jerome was saying, "Don't step in the blood, for Christ's sakes." The house was quiet now, the neighbourhood quiet. A single bang in the night. Nobody would know where it came from. They climbed stairs in the dark. Jerome asked, "You got a flashlight?"

Not that they hadn't had time to plan this thing, Albert was thinking. But he knew if they had sat down cold sober and thought it through, made careful plans, contingencies for when the door was locked, or the Jamaican had a knife, or the power was off, he'd have backed away from it. He would have seen all that could go wrong, and backed the hell off. Instead they were climbing stairs in the dark with a guy bleeding out in the hallway below.

In the first room on the second floor a night-light gave off an eerie glow, revealing a body sprawled on a bed. "Christ," said Albert. "What the hell is this?"

"It's Arlene," said Jerome. "No wonder she didn't leave the door open."

Jerome bent over her. "She's alive. Looks like an overdose or something. Or the cunt's just hammered." He shook her violently. Groggily she opened an eye.

"What was that noise?" she asked, barely moving her lips.

Jerome said, "You stupid cunt. It's your fault he's dead, you know that?'

Arlene said, "Who's dead?"

Albert said, "We got no time for this. Ask her where the money is."

"Who's dead?" She was rousing herself now, taking it in. "Is that you, Jerome?"

"Course it's fucking me."

"Where's Dervon?"

79

"Wha'd'you care where Dervon's at? Where's he keep the money?"

"Is he all right?"

Jerome sat on the bed where her legs were curled. Albert looked at this woman with the heavy eyes and flecks of white on her lips. She had a small chin, spiky hair, a stud coming through her lower lip, an eyebrow ring, a row of small hoops in her left ear. She was wearing a heavy sweater, only panties down below. Her eyes were not taking everything in, something like a Labrador's eyes, thought Albert, not quite understanding but trying to please.

Jerome said, "Where the fuck is your brain, girl? You were supposed to leave the door unlocked."

"Oh." Said Arlene, trying to remember. "Was that tonight?"

"Jesus Christ." Said Albert, but he was suddenly thinking about the time he got wasted and missed his father's funeral. It can happen. Except in this case one guy was dead because of it. Although thinking of the two things at once he realized disappointing his mother was a lot worse than watching Dervon go down.

Jerome was saying, "It was tonight, Sweetie. Now get your pretty little can off the bed and show us where he keeps his money."

"Is Dervon okay?"

"I had to shoot him."

"What?"

"Because of you, Arlene. You remember that. Now get us the fucking money."

"You shot him?"

"That's what I just said."

"That was the noise I heard?" Albert watched her think about this. She opened her mouth to say something else and then changed her mind. Albert watched her. He knew they should be taking what they could, getting the hell out of there. Putting some distance between themselves and this house, and maybe between him and Jerome, but he was watching Arlene do her calculations. They're so fucking good at this, he was thinking.

Albert said to Jerome, "You been played, man."

"What?"

"She didn't leave the door unlocked. She was just waiting to see how it come out. Decide then who she's going with."

Jerome said, "So now she's got no choice. Her man Dervon is bleeding out in the hallway. You hear me Arlene? Where's he keep his money?"

"You taking me with you?" Arlene asked.

"Not much choice," said Jerome. "Either I take you with me or I gotta shoot you. One or the other."

Arlene said, "It's in the sub woofer. He's got this home theatre set up the next room. The sub woofer don't work. Just take the cover off."

Albert stayed with Arlene while Jerome went to look. Arlene said, "I gotta piss badly. Okay if I go to the bathroom?"

Albert said, "Sure." And watched her pull herself off the bed and wobble into the bathroom. She turned on the bathroom light but didn't shut the door. He kept watching her as she pulled down her panties, plopped herself on the toilet, spread her legs a little and smiled up at him. Albert was pretty sure she was saying, "It could be his, it could be yours, whoever takes care of me."

Jerome's Honda Civic was tricked out with a big sound system, a sub in the trunk, right and left in the back corners so Albert had to sit in the middle of the back seat. Arlene sat up front, the bag of money at her feet. She had pulled on jeans, slipped into Italian sandals, thrown some jewellery and cosmetics into an oversized purse and been ready to go. Jerome was driving, Dervon's home theatre projector on the seat next to Albert. When Jerome had come back from the other room, a projector under his arm, Albert had said, "You want I should rent a van we can clean out the place?"

Jerome had missed the sarcasm, said, "Get me a duffle bag or something."

They'd gone out the front door so they didn't have to step over Dervon. Albert wasn't sure what he felt about Dervon, the noise, the shooting, the bleeding, the dying. Maybe he'd feel bad about it later. Right now he was saying, shouting above the bass, "You'll have to ditch the gun."

They were driving down Queensway, heading east, getting a little distance. Jerome shouted back, "Cops don't give a shit a drug house gets robbed."

"They find a body they do." Said Albert.

"There's a 24 hour Timmy's out here," Arlene was saying. "Can we pull in, please, Jerome. I need a coffee real bad."

Albert was surprised when Jerome pulled in at the sign. Jerome said, "We need to stop and think."

Arlene said, "Can we go inside. I'm real cold."

Jerome parked where they could see the car from inside.

When they were sitting with their coffees, about eight sugars in Arlene's, Albert said, "How much you thinks in the bag?"

There were no other customers, maybe an hour away from the very early morning crowd, and all the commuters who'd pull up to the window. Jerome said, "Maybe twenty." Arlene was sitting next to Jerome, leaning into him, making it clear where she was going.

"We should drop your piece in the Welland Canal." Albert said.

"Why? They can't trace it to me. I bought it from some Korean guy for five hundred. Come from Detroit I think."

Albert was thinking, they can trace it if they find it on you, but instead he said, "We need to split up the money and go our separate ways."

"Was a time," Arlene was saying, "you could just show your driver's licence and slip across the border. Try Buffalo for a few months."

"Not going near that fucking border," says Jerome. "Knew a guy crossed with his girlfriend with some mushrooms in the trunk. The Americans put 'em in jail for a week. For a few fucking mushrooms. They're crazy down there. All the shit going on, murder rate ten times any other civilized country, soldiers getting shot up in Iraq, threatening to nuke any God damn place they feel like, and they're arresting pot users, you make any sense of that, and Vietnam deserters, from forty years ago, you read about it, some poor fuck raises his family in Canada, they got a warrant for his arrest for avoiding going to Vietnam 40 years ago, like time didn't prove once an' for all that it was not a fucking good idea to go to war in Vietnam."

Albert recognized the thing happening, said, "Take it easy buddy, time to keep cool. Chill a little." Jerome had just pulled out his piece and shot Dervon point blank, put his piece away, stepped over the body and gone looking for Arlene, cool as a cucumber, but it catches up, even to a hard case like Jerome. He was running on Adrenalin. Albert said, "We ain't going near the States. We need to circle back into Hamilton, go to your place, divvie up the money and scatter. You can keep the projector. I may go out to Vancouver a while."

"They got a nude beach out there," said Arlene.

Jerome said, "Now that is important information, Arlene. We really fucking need to know that right now."

"So we got a plan, right?" Albert intervened. "We go to your place, divide up and split."

"Who the fuck are you, telling me what to do?"

"It's okay man. It's cool. You decide. It's your thing. I just think we…"

"Stop fucking thinking then. I got it covered. We circle back to my place. Finish your coffee before that psycho gets here." Jerome was watching a guy in the parking lot. A guy wearing an old raincoat, a dark toque pulled low, negotiating his way to the door. Doing some sort

84

of three-step. Three steps forward, two to the side, stop, forward again, in these jerky movements, his hair sticking out under the toque, getting to Tim's like he was crossing a rocky stream. "Look at him willya. I think the fucker's talking to himself. "

"He's talking to Jesus," said Arlene, "Might be getting good advice."

"We need to get out of here," said Albert. "He gets in here, makes a scene, they gotta call the cops."

That was the moment the guy stopped, raised his head and shouted something skyward, then stepped rapidly sideways, right to the passenger door of Jerome's Civic, smashed the window with a brick they hadn't seen him pick up, reached in, grabbed the bag sitting on the floor.

"Jesus, shit," said Jerome, half out of his seat.

Jerome was out of there fast. Arlene just sat there staring, not reacting. Albert moved slowly. He felt like he was watching an episode of COPS. Just a spectator, seeing this thing unfold under the lights of the parking lot. The girl behind the counter had heard the smashing window, watched Jerome run out, she was saying, "Should I call the police?"

"Nah, don't bother," said Albert. "Insurance will cover it. The guy's obviously nuts. No big deal. My buddy'll get his bag back."

When Albert got outside, one eye watching the counter girl, making sure she didn't pick up the phone, he could see the Raincoat Guy in the middle of the street, running between the traffic, which was now picking up in the first soft light, commuters flying by, ignoring the

Raincoat Guy. Jerome was following on this side of the road, trying to get across.

Albert was thinking, he catches up to him he'll shoot him right there, cause an accident, dozens of cops arriving. Jerome and the Raincoat Guy were running east. Arlene was still in Timmy's staring into her coffee. The Civic with the smashed window sat in the parking lot. Jerome had the key. Albert watched for a few more minutes. The Raincoat Guy was not slowing down. Jerome was weaving his way across three lanes, getting to the middle, and the Raincoat Guy was dashing across the lanes going the other way. Albert was losing sight of them behind the big trucks on the highway. He was wondering if the psycho bit was fake. If the guy knew the bag was full of money. Only one way that could have happened, he figured. It was Arlene wanted to stop at this Tim Horton's. She could be playing it three ways. Or else this guy is just a junkie, does a smash and grab hoping for something he can pawn for a little medicine. Doesn't know he's running with a bag of cash.

Either way, Albert figured. If Arlene set this up then she's two steps ahead of us and it's time to give up, and if this junkie just happens to be at this Tim Horton's at this precise time in the morning, and the Civic just happens to be the only car in the lot, and he's just doing a routine he's done many times before…. Means you're either up against a real smart woman or somebody fixed the dice.

Albert took one last look at Arlene. She wasn't moving, calmly waiting to see how this played out. The counter girl was watching Arlene and cars were starting to pull up to the window. Jerome was getting pretty small way down the highway on the other side, going east. He couldn't see the Raincoat Guy anymore.

Hands in his pockets, head bowed against the wind, Albert began the long walk back to downtown Hamilton.

10

Give me back my broken night

No matter what happens during the day around Lake Ontario, whether it's early winter or Indian summer, six in the morning is always cold in late October. Albert had not dressed for a long walk down King Street, from the east end to James. That was a fucking bust, he was thinking. He kicked at a Tim Horton's cup lying on the sidewalk. Nothing ever works out. He should know. And now this Arlene chick, how was she going to play it? He should figure this out. By the time he gets back he should figure this out. A light fog from the lake haloed the lingering street lamps as Albert pulled his collar up.

She could identify him as the guy with Jerome. But then Jerome could tell the cops how she set the whole thing up. Or she could just play dumb. Say she was stoned and didn't know what the fuck was going on. And Jerome. He manages to catch up with the Raincoat Guy and get the bag of money back without a lot of cops arriving and he gets back to Horton's and sees Albert's taken off and still no cops – then everything's cool. He's got twenty grand to himself, and maybe Arlene. But if he doesn't catch the Raincoat Guy and comes back to Timmy's, sees Albert's taken off, then he'll be some pissed. Or the cops pick them both up and link them to Dervon.

Or the cops are there already cause the girl called them, and Arlene's telling her story. But Arlene looks smarter than that. Wouldn't cop to anything until she knows who's got the twenty grand.

Albert's head hurt from trying to think this through. Too many variables. He should probably do what he usually does: Ignore it all. It didn't fucking happen.

He kept walking, through those pathetic black arches into the downtown core. Hock shops, sex shops, money marts, falafel places, whole blocks boarded up, new lampposts though. Even the Sand Bar was looking desolate, ever since the cops confiscated the property. My kind of town. The wind blew down King against him, pushing damp air at his face.

The image of Dervon bleeding out kept coming into his mind. Shit. Up to now he'd had a few drug busts, no big deal. But even if Dervon was a low life scum, there just weren't enough murders in this town for the cops to ignore this one. Maybe in Baltimore. What the hell is another dead dealer in Baltimore? Detroit? But here the newspaper will headline it as number five or six for the year and the cops will feel obliged to look into it seriously. They'll find Arlene for sure. And she can finger Jerome. And he could point to Albert. Best to not think too hard about it.

He could use a hit of something so fucking bad now. But his appointment with his PO was coming up. Might be out of his system by then. But he takes one hit, he'll go for more, test positive, get breached. The usual. Had told himself this time'd be different. At least five times leading up to this mess he could have walked away. Kept walking when he ran into Jerome. No big deal. What the hell was wrong with him letting an asshole like Jerome get him into this mess? As he trudged along King Street he wondered it wasn't the money, or the crime, the

89

excitement. He wondered if the problem was fear. He could have gotten on some subsidized training thing, gone back to school, looked for a winter job. He could have planned the next year or two, like Sam kept pushing. But there was Jerome saying, nah, you don't have to worry about all that bullshit, just come for a ride with me.

Round the corner, going north on James, past the hole in the ground where the old Tivoli Theatre used to be, hands in his pockets, head down, walking fast, he almost tripped over the guy. The guy getting up from the sidewalk, levering himself with a bottle in a brown bag, now up and coming behind him. Talking.

"Where you going so fast? Albert, man."

Albert turned when he heard his name, slowed a little. He recognized Billy in the poor light. Missing teeth, scabby skin, must have shaved with a broken bottle, spent the night out. Black hair parted in the middle. Hands cut up and a little shaky.

Billy was talking fast, catching up to Albert. "You got a little change on you? I wouldn't be asking 'cept I could be in big trouble. McIntire's a judge now, you know that, asked me I have anything to do with firebombing that lawyer's office over on Herkimer. Cocksucker. You know how it is. I told him it had nothing to do with me."

Only a few blocks from his apartment Albert didn't want Billy following him there, seeing where he lived. He had to stop and listen. He had no idea what the guy was talking about, a firebombing. But Billy changed the subject, went on about being kicked out of the Mission, couldn't go back for 72 hours, a bullshit rule, but what would you have done? "This guy was telling me he finds where my old lady

90

lives he's gonna do my girls. You believe that shit. I had to set 'im straight. So what do you think? You got maybe five bucks?"

Albert said, "You could try the Sally Ann." He was getting cold, just standing there, shoulders pulled in.

"Same fucking bullshit. Not for 48 hours. How about ten bucks then, something to get me warm? Just a loan, man. I'm good for it."

In the joint Billy could rant about his old lady and kids for hours. Always wanting to get back with them, blaming the doctors and lawyers for busting up his happy home. Mean and unpredictable, this Billy. He'd give him five bucks he had it on him, get rid of him for now, ignore the fact Billy'd be on him everyday after that. He turns and walks, Billy'd be after him, following him. And having Billy behind you was not a good thing.

He said, "Look, man. I got nothing on me, but I got something better than that. I'm gonna give you an address. You get there fast you can just walk in and get lots a stuff to trade. Electronics, blue jeans."

"You're bullshitting."

"No. Guaranteed. Back door's open. Go in and help yourself."

"No fucking way. You're brushing me off. Like that fucking McIntire."

Albert could see Billy's eyes move from suspicion to greed and back again. He said, "Suit yourself," and turned to walk away.

"No. Wait a minute. What is this place you're talking about?"

Albert called over his shoulder, "It's a house. Lotta good stuff inside. Owner don't need it no more. Two fifty-six Wentworth. Two fifty-six."

Albert kept walking. He walked past the entrance to the stairs up to his place before he looked back. Billy had turned and was heading in the right direction at a good clip. Albert smiled to himself before going back to the doorway. He could picture Billy stumbling over Dervon. He might find some of Dervon's stash and still be there when the cops arrive, even a day later. They probably wouldn't like Billy for it, but he'd sure mess up the crime scene.

11

Your private life will suddenly explode

Albert slept most of the day, got up to piss a few times, rummaged in the small refrigerator looking for some beer he knew he didn't have, crawled back in bed, ignored the street sounds. Down below his window, the old wops would be standing around outside the coffee shops and clubs, the Chinese or Vietnamese or whatever they were, putting boxes of Bok Choy out on the sidewalks, the guys from the Mission kicked out at eight after breakfast, walking by looking for butts, heading up town for the warmth of the Mall. There'd been some robberies in the neighbourhood, and a couple of late night shootings past few weeks, outside the café used to be owned by the Musitanos. Who knew what the fuck was going on there now? Crips up against the oriental gangs, bikers poaching on the Jamaicans' territory, like there wasn't enough crack or meth business to go around.

He'd read the Musitano brothers were getting out soon. Albert wondered if they'd come back to their old stomping grounds, walk up and down James, wondered if they'd have anything going for them after being away for five years and coming out on pretty tight parole. Nothing used to go down in this neighbourhood without the Musitanos knowing about it. Maybe they'd have the same PO. Pat, his brother, and Albert all checking in with Sam. Good looking woman, that Sam.

Dervon's face intruded on his thoughts. He hadn't actually seen the guy's face in the dark hallway, but now in his half dream the man was lying there, bleeding from a chest wound, mouth leaking red froth, eyes wide open, staring up at Albert saying the words, "What the fuck?" over and over. Albert turned his thoughts to doing it with Sam, went back to sleep before he got her blouse off.

He didn't know what time the knocking on his door woke him up. He ignored it, couldn't be anything good. God damn property guy collecting rent, which he was only behind one month, which he figured was fair because of how late they were turning the heat on in the building. The knocking was not loud like a rent collector though, or police, or the husband of some woman he might or might not have done. And then some sounds he couldn't interpret, like a body leaning against his door and sliding down and thumping on the floor. That got him out of bed but he veered to the bathroom first, pissed and pulled his pants on, before slipping the dead bolt and opening his door.

She was there, sitting on the floor, leaning against the doorframe, slowly looking up at him. She said, "You got anything to drink?"

Albert turned away from the door, found a shirt hanging on the back of a chair, pulled it on. She closed the door behind her and sat in the one good chair, looked around. Albert found himself looking with her, seeing the place through her eyes. A shit hole one bedroom apartment he'd been living in six months without broom or vacuum, couple of windows looking over James, clothes scattered here and there, open suitcase with the rest, kitchen table with newspapers, used bowls, cups, fast food wrappers, small kitchen, living room, a bathroom, bedroom, paint over wallpaper on the walls, one old ratty carpet, nice new plasma TV and DVD player looking out-of place in the otherwise forty year old decor. She was looking at the TV.

"I got it cheap. I think it fell off the back of a truck," Albert said. He didn't know why he needed to explain his one luxury. She wandered into the kitchen, looking around. He sat straddling one of the two kitchen chairs, smoothed his hair. He needed a shower, but he wanted to know what Arlene had to say. He waited for her. Noticed it was getting dark. About six, six-thirty.

But she wasn't saying anything, just looking at him. Albert asked, "How'd you find me?"

"Asked around," she said. "Wasn't hard."

"Okay," said Albert. "You gonna tell me or let me guess? What happened? Jerome come back with the money? What?"

"The counter girl called her supervisor, who was probably gonna call the cops, so I left."

"The Raincoat Guy. You know him?"

"What?"

"I mean was it just dumb luck he picks that Civic, grabs that bag, that what you're telling me?"

"You're asking something, ask it straight out."

"Okay. Do you know the Raincoat Guy? Did you set the whole thing up?"

"I know who he might be. Dervon used to sell to him, when he had some change. But no way did I set that up. Why would I do that? Jerome promised me half."

"That and a buck twenty-four will buy you a medium regular." He was trying to remember if Jerome had promised him half or he had just assumed half for himself, and half for himself and half for Jerome plus Arlene's half didn't leave much. The usual bullshit. Until you got it in your pocket, man, it ain't nothing. "So next straight question. Why'd you come here?"

"I've got no place else to go. You and Jerome kinda screwed up Dervon's place for me."

Albert waited for it.

Arlene looked away. She said, "Let me use your bathroom." Albert nodded his head. She got up, got halfway there, then said, over her shoulder, as if an afterthought, "I might know where we can find your Raincoat Guy."

When she finally came out of the bathroom she acted as if she owned the place, walked and talked like her name was on the lease. Told Albert the bathroom needed some attention, like maybe a team of Molly Maids could bring it back to third world standards. She stretched out in the one soft chair in the living room, took the remote and turned on his plasma TV. Told him she'd been on the street all day, would he be a hon', and go fetch some Kentucky Fried or something. Swiss Chalet up at the corner.

He watched her from the kitchen. The thing she said before going into the bathroom held him. He said, "Are you clean?"

She said, flipping channels, "Just washed my hands, sugar."

"You know what I mean."

"Three months."

"Living with Dervon, how'd you manage that?"

"Maybe a lapse or two, but it was coming. Why I had to get away. CAS's got my kid and I'm trying to get her back. I need a place of my own. Gotta test clean, go to counselling, anger management, the whole thing. That ten grand would come in handy. I get settled I get to see my baby again."

"You said you might know where the Raincoat Guy's at. You don't think Jerome caught up to him?"

"I doubt it."

"So the Raincoat Guy and the twenty grand? Where do you think?"

"I haven't eaten all day, Hon. Whyn't you go get us something? I might even clean up around here while you're gone."

He couldn't see her lugging out his Plasma TV on her own, and there was nothing else in the apartment worth stealing, so he shrugged, put on his jacket. "Swiss Chalet's closer than KFC, or some Chinese takeout, maybe."

"Whatever," she said. "Just so's it's fast. Some diet Coke too. Please."

The "Please" was offered with a nice little seductive tilt of her head, so Albert smiled, put a jacket on, and left his apartment.

In the hallway, before the stairs leading down to the street, he passed Harry's door, heard this rough baritone voice, slurring a little, saying, repeating, working out something, "Ponds and Aspen, thick with the muttering of insect life. It is, like love, a flickering abundance." And, "What romantic horseshit."

The Honda Civic with the smashed window was parked on James, just down from Jerry's Man Shop. Albert saw it and stopped, suddenly wary and feeling guilty. Man, he hated himself for that. It was his thinking about going in with Arlene and doing Jerome out of the twenty grand that did it to him. And he hadn't even decided to do it yet. Like he owed Jerome anything. Fucker says there's gonna be no violence and then he shoots a guy. He didn't owe Jerome shit. Still, he waited, looked around. The Civic was empty. The usual street scene, young Italians or Portuguese watching the women walking by, which weren't much I'll tell ya, especially you count the bag lady in the long overcoat picking through the trash, carrying her findings in a shopping bag, a couple of drunks doing the wide step.

Jerome was off somewhere, one of the bars maybe. Maybe looking for his buddy Albert who had walked on him, left him talking to the police alone.

Albert hurried past the empty Civic, crossed the street and entered the Crystal Palace Flowering Dynasty or whatever the hell it was, the Chinese joint advertising Vancouver Crab $9.99.

On his way back, bag of Chinese take out under his arm he walked a few extra blocks, skirting James Street, going west a couple of blocks to Bay and down Bay to Barton and then coming back up, avoiding the bars and Jerome. He hardly recognized the place when he got back, everything tidied up, the table cleared off, two plates set on it, with clean forks and glasses, the sink empty, dishes put away.

She looked at him when he came in, some of her makeup off, hair a little wilder, standing in his kitchen.

He said, "What are we? The ……." He was trying to think of a sitcom with the wife at home in the kitchen and Dad comes home from work bringing the chicken or pizza, but nothing came to mind except The Waltons, which he said, which didn't really fit the bill. She looked at him curiously, then said, "That doesn't smell like Kentucky Fried."

He put the large bag of white boxes on the table, draped his jacket over a chair and went to the bathroom to wash his hands, which he knew was unusual and recognized it as an old habit – he'd come to the table as a kid and his mother would simply give him that look and he'd go wash his hands before dinner. Just standing there in a clean kitchen, Arlene watching him, that kicked it in. When he came out, she'd emptied a couple of cartons into bowls, the others still in their white boxes. She was sitting at the table waiting.

She said, "You only have two bowls."

He said, "When I'm having a big party I have it catered."

She had an appetite, piling it on her plate, shovelling it in. He started eating faster, getting that boarding house twinge. He told her, "Jerome's busted Civic is parked a few blocks up the street. He may be looking for me, or you."

She paused, "He's probably looking for me, or the Raincoat Guy, not you. What can you do for him?"

Albert took another mouthful of Beef with Oyster Sauce. "He's got no reason to be pissed at me. Anybody would have walked from that debacle."

She said, "De-bacal?"

He said, "It means, you know, a fucking mess."

"I know what it means. Just a word I don't hear much. 'Fucking mess' I hear a lot."

He put his fork down, looked at her, waited.

She said, "I think the Raincoat Guy's got a room at the Regal. I think he'd go back there."

Albert didn't ask how she might know this. He said, "Okay. So he gets away. Let's say he gets away. Say he doesn't toss the bag when he's running. Say he looks in it, sees cash, what's he gonna do then?"

She said, "I don't think he's gonna make a down payment on a house. He's a small buyer, a few bucks at a time, a piece of rock, out hustling, comes back with a few more bucks. That's his pattern. Spends the day hustling for pennies, gets enough, makes a buy, gets high. People don't change."

"He might get some big ideas he sees all that money, go in business for himself."

"No. I think more likely he'll try making a bigger buy, flash the money around, get himself mugged, or overdose on some pure shit, not used to anything hasn't been cut. But first he'll take the money back to his room, spread it out on his bed, and run his hands through it."

"That's what you think?"

"Absolutely."

"How do you know that?'

"Cause it's what I'd do."

Albert thought about that for a minute. Yeah, you'd want to touch it. If it was a million you'd pile it in one place and look at it. Twenty thousand in small bills you'd spread it out. He said, "Whatever he does, it'll be gone pretty fast."

She said, "Yeah, so probably we should get some sleep, and then go visit him before the sun comes up."

Albert said, "You got this thing all planned, huh?"

It was five A.M. she woke him up, pushed him out of bed. She was already dressed. Pulling on his pants, he said, "So what's the plan? We just gonna knock on his door, ask him to please hand us the money?"

She said, "I think we'll need something to persuade him."

"Well, I'm telling you now," Albert said. "I don't do guns. I just don't do 'em."

"I've seen the guy. He's wasted. There's no muscle on him at all. "

"You figure I can just take him, bare hands?"

"No. Your job is to distract him. I want him watching you when I mace him. Then you can take him."

"You got mace?"

"Some pretty good pepper spray should do it." She grabbed her purse, pulled out a spray can, flashed it briefly to Albert, put it back.

"That stuff legal?" he asked.

She said, pulling on one of his two jackets, "Pretty much."

Going out the door, Albert said, grinning, "Don't think I could handle being the distraction I wasn't so secure in my manhood." There was no voice coming from Harry's door this time.

Walking up James and over to Bay in the still dark October morning, Albert looked over at Arlene as they passed under a street lamp. She was five seven or so, one of his oversize jackets on her, determined look on her face, walking fast beside him. She'd been a surprise last night, cleaning up the dishes, wiping the counter, coming out of the bathroom and just crawling all over him, telling him to be quiet, men talk too much. Giving him the best blow job he'd had in months. And him lying there knowing this woman had it all figured out, this being just a down payment to get him cooperative. But, what the hell? She sure warmed up his dismal one bedroom.

"How are we getting in the Regal, by the way?"

"Are you kidding? Back door'll be propped open. How else the buyers gonna come and go."

"You know what floor he's on? What room?"

"Uh huh."

"How do you know this?"

"I tracked him down yesterday. Before I found you."

"How the hell you do that?"

"I describe him, tell them he's my brother, living on the street, and I gotta find him on account our mother is dying. Didn't take long."

Albert wondered if that was all there was to it. Maybe. He moved ahead of her, walking backwards for a few paces, looking her in the eye.

She didn't say anything, kept walking. Albert fell in beside her, said, "That's okay. That's good. That's cool."

The streets were empty, a cold wind coming straight at them, for the walk west past the Sally Ann across from the market and the old Eaton Centre, now home to surplus outlets. A few trucks were on the road already, some cars starting the early commute to Toronto. They crossed Bay, and then an empty wind-swept parking lot, coming in on the alley behind the Regal. She was right. The back door had been jammed with a small brick and the light over the door was out. The building was three stories, old brick on the corner, with a street level façade of barn-boards and an old faded sign reading 'Beers From Around the World', like the guys who drank in this dive cared what flavours their alcohol came in. With each incarnation, signs had been hastily erected, remnants of previous names left visible, but the one constant was the tavern on the main floor, once called the Regal and forever known as The Regal no matter the creative re-branding of new owners. There was a coffee place out front with a sign that had been there maybe three years announcing a grand opening, Genuine Columbian, but never opened. Albert figured it had to be a way to wash a bit of drug money. He guessed most of the guys who had rooms here were barred from the Mission and the Sally Ann and were just waiting to go back to jail.

As he followed Arlene into the piss-smelling ground floor hall, Albert was thinking there was a bit of irony here. Jerome had talked him into the thing right here, drinking Canadian on tap at Beers From Around the World. He's gotta start hanging out with a classier bunch of people.

She led the way up a back flight of stairs to the second floor hallway, old linoleum, wooden doors, that cheesy smell of something hadn't been cleaned in years. She stopped in front of a door numbered eleven, the number painted in black right on the wood. He flattened himself against the wall. She knocked, waited. She knocked again. Albert heard some movement this time. Again she knocked, this time saying, "It's me, Arlene. Open up Charley, honey. It's just me."

He caught that. She knew his name, the Raincoat Guy. He'd have to think about that. She was saying, "Charley, baby. It's cold out here. I'm freezing my tits off. C'mon now. Open the fucking door."

A voice from inside called out something like, "Wait a minute. Just wait a Goddamn minute. Jesus H. Christ."

Albert could hear him moving around, either putting on his clothes, hiding the money, or hiding his chemicals.

The door opened a crack. All the Raincoat Guy could see was Arlene. He opened it more, and Albert pushed it wide and stepped in, Arlene beside him. This Charley was tall and gaunt like Arlene said, with real bad teeth, sores on his face, eyes waking up, getting that paranoid stare. He was muttering, "What the fuck. What the fuck. You said you were alone." He looked from Albert to Arlene and Arlene was looking him right in the face and saying, "I lied, Sweetie," as she reached quickly into her purse and brought out the can and got him square in his dirty eyes.

The guy was howling now, his hands up to his face, reeling back, and Albert dove at him, briefly wishing he'd worn gloves.

Albert wasn't good at this. They were falling over the one chair in the room, onto the side of the bed, knocking a small table over, crashing to the floor, this Charley surprisingly strong, blinded but struggling like mad, and Albert just trying to hold him down, the guy now trying to get under the bed, pull himself under the bed, and Albert pulling him back, and the guy, breath like rotten cabbage, actually getting on top of Albert for a moment and then a smashing sound and he slumps all over Albert, a bit of blood and spittle hitting Albert in the face.

Pushing him off, Albert could see the shattered ceramic lamp she'd hit him with.

"Christ, he's filthy." Albert was saying as he got out from under the dead weight, and brushed himself off, wiping his face of spit and blood, on his jacket sleeve, keeping it from his mouth and eyes. She had calmly closed the door and was standing there, waiting for him.

She said, "You aren't much good at this, are you?"

There was a sink in the room, clothes scattered, pop cans, food containers, socks, general shit, the bed hastily made. Albert went to the sink, turned a tap and splashed water on his face. He said, "He isn't HIV positive, is he?"

She was looking at the bed. "See that. I told you what he'd do. He's been sleeping with it."

Albert looked up from the sink. He could see a lone crumpled bill peeking out from under the top bed sheet.

Arlene whipped the one blanket and sheet back. A stench rose up from the yellowing bed. But she had been right. The bottom sheet was spread with piles of crumpled bills, mostly twenties, some fifties and hundreds.

"I think he whacked off on them," Albert said, gingerly picking up a few.

Arlene grabbed a pillowcase, told Albert to start filling it. He was careful at first, then told himself he'd scrub his hands once he got back home. He filled the pillowcase and Arlene double bagged it, tied a knot at the end. Charley was still out, but breathing, making a noise with his face on the floor. Arlene said, "Leave him a hundred bucks, enough to get high for a while. He'll forget the whole thing."

They'd been pretty thorough, getting every last bill. Albert told her she'd have to undo the knot. She looked at him, said, "Give him one of the bills you put in your pocket." She wasn't upset though, just matter of fact. Albert took a hundred from his pocket and stuffed it in Raincoat Guy's right hand. 'Charley' just didn't fit this bleeding, floppy, stinking, toothless meth-head. Charley being a sort of up-beat name, Albert was thinking.

"Are you coming?" she asked as she opened the door just enough to take a look down the hall.

Albert pulled himself away, glanced around the room before he stepped into the corridor.

The went down the stairs quietly, Albert leading the way, Arlene carrying the pillow case. They could see it was getting light outside when they reached the bottom. But sprawled there just inside the back door, half blocking it, was a lumpy shape, not there when they came in. "Christ," muttered Albert, pulling up short.

"What?"

"Nothing. It's Billy. How ya doing, Billy?"

"Shit man, Albert. That you? Thanks for nothing, man. There was a body there, you know that? A fucking dead guy. I nearly puked. But you should've seen it go up man. The whole place. Took the fire trucks a good twenty minutes to get there, you know that. They pay those fuckers too much." Billy was pulling himself up, using the wall to hold himself, thinking about it, through a haze of something, trying to focus. Before he could put it all together, before he could wonder what the hell Albert and this woman were doing coming down the back stairs of the Regal, Albert reached into his pocket and pulled out a second hundred dollar bill, handed it to Billy. Billy was looking at it. He looked up at Albert. "A hundred's no good to me, man. Nobody'll take a hundred these days. Not from me."

Albert went back into his pocket, pulled out three, four twenties, gave them to Billy and tried to take back the hundred. Billy slumped back down, kept the hundred, said, "This'll do fine, man. This'll do fine."

Arlene pulled him out the door, walking fast, straight down Bay. Going across Cannon she said, "What was that about? The dead guy he was talking about. Wouldn't be Dervon, would it?"

"I'm worried about HIV," Albert said. "You think he was positive?"

"You get it in your mouth, your eyes? You got any cuts?"

"I don't think so."

"So don't worry about it."

They'd gone another block, cars beginning to line up for the early morning Tim Horton's take out, a large double double for the road. He said, "Hep C. He probably has Hep C, right?"

"Just wash your hands when we get back."

He said, "My old man had Hep C, you know that? Wasn't what killed him though."

****

There she was, sitting on the can again, Albert in the shower. She had no modesty, this woman, pissing right there in front of him. He said, scrubbing the Regal off himself, "You think we can wash those bills? I mean, like literally wash them?"

108

She said, "They should be okay we just air them out." She got up, pulled her panties on, her jeans. "You got coffee somewhere I'll make a pot."

He said, "Look in the back of the fridge. Might be some."

When he came out of the bathroom she'd found an old cone filter and was boiling water on the stove. Two mugs, a can of coffee, sugar, a jar of coffee-mate on the counter. She said, "If we're living together you gotta do better than this."

He heard the 'living together' bit, ignored it, sat in one of the chairs, said, "I think that shit was left by the previous tenant."

The pillowcase full of money was sitting on the kitchen table in front of him, the street getting noisy down below. He said, "I hate to touch the stuff."

"Coffee?"

"No. I mean the money. It's gotta be filthy. He was rolling in it for Christ's sake."

"You're so fucking sensitive. I'll count it." She put a mug of coffee in front of him, the coffee-mate and a bowl of sugar.

He said, "I usually just go downstairs get a cup, a cappuccino or something."

She was grappling with the knot, trying not to break a fingernail, when she was stopped by a knocking on the door, not a knocking, more like an open hand patting. Then a voice outside saying, "Albert boy, you in there? You got something for me? I am in the throes of deprivation, Albert."

She said, "Who the hell is that?"

109

Albert got up from his chair. "It's Harry. My neighbour. He's harmless. He's just a sad old drunk. It's not coffee he's after, though."

When Albert opened the door, Harry almost fell in. He had a suit jacket on over a frayed white shirt, a poor tie. His clothes seemed a little big for him. When he brought his hand up to his face Albert noticed the tremor. He said, "Jesus Harry, you're not looking so good."

"I'm in the demon withdrawal," said Harry, unsteadily moving past Albert towards the kitchen table. "Let me sit awhile."

The pillowcase of money was no longer on the table. Arlene was standing at the counter pouring another cup of coffee.

Harry took a kitchen chair, saying, "You have company, Albert. Don't let me stay and bother you."

'It's all right, Harry. Sit awhile. This is Arlene."

Arlene said, "Hi, Harry." And leaned against the counter, suddenly less friendly.

Albert reached high and into the back of the cupboard over the stove. He came out with a twenty-six of rum three quarters full.

Arlene said, "We could have used that last night."

Pouring about three ounces into a glass, Albert said, "I keep this for Harry. I hide it back there so I forget about it and I only bring it out in emergencies. This looks like an emergency, Harry." He put the glass on the table in front of Harry.

Harry looked at it a minute, like he was testing himself, or not wanting to appear too desperate. Then he reached for it, had trouble closing his fingers on it, and then the tremors worsened, and he was splashing on the way to his lips, and spilling a little down his chin.

110

Arlene, suddenly softened, said, "Here, Sweetie, lemme do it." She took the glass from his hand and held it steadily, tilting it just right on Harry's lower lip. He sipped gingerly, politely, until the glass was empty. His eyes went to the bottle on the counter and Albert poured him another three ounces.

When the second glass was empty and Albert didn't move to fill it again, Harry rested his hands on the table, said, "That's better. You're a gentleman, Albert, and your lady's a lady. I am very contrite. I am not usually so helpless. Please forgive me. Perhaps I'll be able to write a little before the tremors start again."

As he got up from his chair, Harry said, with a little bow, "I'm very pleased to meet you, Arlene. A young man should not go through life alone. We are helpless creatures without a woman's touch." He made his way to the door, said, "Nor an old man for that matter."

When the door was closed behind Harry, Arlene said, "You really keep that rum for Harry?"

"He tries to stop, you know, but I don't want to see him in D.T.'s, so I keep it handy."

"You're surprising, Albert." She went into the bathroom to get the pillowcase out of the tub, where she'd quickly dumped it when Albert let Harry in.

Talking to her back as she walked away, Albert said, "It was my old man. Same thing. You know. When I was a kid, he'd get in pretty rough shape, he couldn't find his bottle, or mom had ditched it. I'd find it for him. He was a mean drunk though. Not like Harry. Harry's the same, drunk or sober. A professor or something. A poet. I think he's published a book or two years ago. That's what he's doing in there, writing poetry, you believe it?"

"Now this is poetry," she said, dumping the contents of the pillowcase on the table.

Looking at it, Albert said, "We keep this we gotta figure out what to do with Jerome, you know that."

Arlene settled in a chair counting and piling. Albert said, "And your buddy Charley. He may come looking for us too."

She said, "I think there's over twenty thousand here."

12

Your servant here, he has been told

He'd left her with the money to make his appointment with Sam. Stuffed a couple of thousand into his pockets first. She asked him what he was doing. He'd told her it was insurance. She's gone when he gets back he's still got a little to show for his troubles. She had said, "I'll still be here."

She was still there when he got back, carrying an LCBO bag with a bottle of cheap rum in it. She had a newspaper open to the classified on the kitchen table, a few listings circled. "The rum's for Harry," he said.

"Here's the deal," she had told him before he left to see his PO. "I have to rent a decent place to get my daughter back. You need to move before Jerome gives up looking for me, or Charley, and comes looking for you. So we get a place together, two bedroom, Mr. and Mrs., we give first and last in cash. You can stay or not. It's up to you. We just need to figure out a reference."

"A reference?"

"You know. Someone to vouch we're a nice young couple, pay our rent on time."

So Albert brought back a bottle for Harry to convince him to pose as a landlord and give them a good reference. And what started as a simple partnership in a heist with Jerome seemed to be changing into a marriage. Albert remembered the conversation he had had with

113

Jerome, Jerome telling him he should give into his nature, go with the flow, stop trying to plan and control. And look where it got him. Now it was his only option, just go with it, see where it takes him. He was looking at Arlene, wondering how such a clever, scheming woman could get herself caught up with a black guy dealing out of a house on Wentworth. He asked, "How old is your kid?"

"She's six. Started grade one this year."

"And the father?"

"What about the father?"

"You didn't get this kid on your own. There's gotta be a father someplace."

"He's not part of it. And the kid has a name. Wave."

"Wave?"

"Yes, Wave."

"Wave like in wave goodbye?"

"No. Wave as in white caps curling on a beach."

Albert thought about that for a minute. Then he said, "That's a hippy sort of name. A tree hugger thing."

She said, "I was very young at the time, and I hated my own name. *Arlene*. How boring can you get?"

"And the Children's Aid have her."

"Yeah. And they're gonna go for permanent custody if I don't pretty soon prove to them I can make a home for her."

Albert looked around the apartment. Cleaned up and tidy. Arlene quite pretty sitting there at this table, his table, a young mother, sadness in her eyes talking about Wave. You take away the lip ring and the tongue stud, maybe half the earrings, soften up the hair spikes.....

"Okay," he said. "I'll talk with Harry and then we go look at a couple of places. But we still got one major problem. Maybe two major problems."

She said, "Jerome. He's not gonna give up on his twenty grand that easy. But Charley. I wouldn't worry about Charley."

Albert decided he better worry about both Jerome and Charley, but he took the bottle down the hall to Harry.

As he left the apartment she said, "What is it with you and Harry, anyway?"

He stopped, considered this. She said, "None of my business. But you keep a bottle specially for him. You're pretty sure he'll lie for you."

He stood there, thinking about her question, how to answer it.

She said, "You can tell me later. If you want to."

13

Take the only tree that's left

Jerome sat in the Regal alone, watching the door. He'd been asking around for Arlene, but he couldn't make it too obvious, have it get to the cops. They were both gone when he'd gotten back to Horton's, the Honda with the smashed window sitting there, the projector on the back seat. By ten he'd pawned the projector, got two hundred for it, but he still had the gun, weighing heavily in his belt, screaming at him. He knew he should get rid of it. But it really pissed him he was empty handed. That he'd shot a guy for nothing.

The wino in the rain coat, ran like the fucking wind, would you believe it. Jerome was edgy, couldn't think what to do but wait. Wait for someone to come in that door knew where his twenty grand was. Him and Wally the only patrons this early, pathetic. Gave him time to look the place over. Some guy was really into shit green they painted this place. The guy behind the bar had a pouchy face and tattoos up both arms.

Then the guy comes in, the mean one, the one with the eyes, usually begging in the mall this guy, someone you walk around, does his time in solitary when he's in. The one who's always going on about some doctor talked his wife into leaving him. He gets a chance he shows a picture of a woman and two young kids, dug out of his pockets with an old driver's licence, health card, plastic social security,

116

receipts, scraps, papers, cards, forms, all torn and weathered on the edges. William, Bill, something. Not the Raincoat Guy, too short. While Jerome's watching him, this guy goes to the bar, waves some money around. Couple of twenties. Not much, but a guy like him doesn't usually have twenties, coins and fives maybe, but not twenties. Wally's noticed this as well, and is heading towards the guy. Wally, talking to himself, don't seem to notice anything, unless it's the possibility of a free drink. He gets to the guy, stands a couple of feet from him. The guy says something to Wally. Wally retreats to his corner. The guy's missing a couple of teeth, scabs on his face, stubble, but what there is of him is probably muscle. The kinda guy you buy the drinks for and you got a friend for an hour or two, learn anything you want. You stop buying for him he turns on you.

Jerome should wait. He doesn't know for sure there's a connection. But he wants his money; he's been all over the town looking, he's tired of looking. So the first time he sees this guy head for the washroom he gets up and follows. Wally watches from the corner, muttering to himself.

The guy is standing at the urinal when Jerome comes in. The guy is starting to turn but Jerome moves fast. His left arm across the back of the guy's head, pushing him forward, the gun out and the muzzle stuck in his side. The guy not saying anything yet. Then, "You fucker. Made me piss down my pants."

From the smell, Jerome figures it's not the first time he pissed down his pants. He says, "Just tell me something. I don't want your money. Nothing. Just tell me where you got it."

"Where I got what?"

"The money you're flashing around."

"Investments," says Billy, his head against the cold water pipes.

Jerome pushes on him, says, "I didn't say I wouldn't shoot your fucking balls off."

Billy says, "Guy give it to me."

Thing was, it was a situation this asshole's got a gun in his side, no help coming in this place, he should just tell him what he wants and get clear, but that wouldn't be right. That wouldn't be fair, and fairness is important to Billy.

"What guy?" says Jerome.

"A guy. Just a fucking guy. Will you get off my neck?"

"He got a name, this guy?"

"Course he's got a fucking name. His mommy give it to him."

Billy's face is still up against the cold pipes. Jerome raises his arm to hit him in the back of the head with the butt of his gun. But Billy turns in time to catch Jerome's wrist. Jerome was right. This guy is short and ugly but he's all muscle. For a second they're standing there in front of the urinal, in a stalemate. Billy's fly is still open, his cock hanging out. This distracts Jerome just long enough for Billy to bring his knee up, catching Jerome in the groin. Jerome starts to buckle over. He sees Billy's face in the hard glare of washroom light. He remembers him from the lock up, used to keep this guy in his cell on Three B, twenty-four seven. Mean little bastard. He oughta shoot him right here, but he wouldn't be lucky twice. Jerome backs away. He says, pointing the gun at Billy's chest, "I don't want your money. I don't want nothing from you 'cept a name. Who gave you the fucking money?"

Billy doesn't seem to even notice the gun. He's got that look on his face, eyes scanning, a little grin, pupils dilated. He says, "You got anything to do with the thing went down on Wentworth couple days ago?"

Jerome's got the gun on Billy. He's still buckled over, starting to straighten up. He's figuring this out. Billy's grinning at him, saying, "You're one sorry fuck, you know that."

And that's the moment the Raincoat Guy comes in. He stops just inside the door, by the overflowing white trash can. Jerome's still buckled over, watching Billy. Raincoat Guy doesn't see Jerome's face right away. His left eye is swollen shut, blood still crusted to his matted hair. He's squinting at Billy with his right eye when he says, "Did I fucking interrupt something? "

14

You don't know me from the wind

The door to Albert's apartment was open when they got back from looking at townhouses, two bedroom apartments.

It had been a unique experience for Albert, going though kitchens, bedrooms, bathrooms, with Arlene, the assumption growing as they enacted it, the naturalness of being a couple checking appliances, plumbing, closet space, neighbourhood. Even asking about schools, bus routes, shopping. They had a six year old, Arlene told the landladies, the property managers. Albert tilted his head and raised his eyebrows the first time, but after that he went with it. He didn't have much to say about any of the townhouses, each being an improvement over his own apartment. Arlene made up for his silence, trying taps and stoves and looking in refrigerators, asking questions of the landlady, occasionally taking his arm and saying, "There's a perfect spot for your big TV."

They carried the twenty-three thousand four hundred dollars with them, half each in fanny packs Arlene bought at the dollar store. It's a nice chunk of change to have in his possession, Albert was thinking, but he was aware he and a couple of friends could run through it in a weekend. Or, he could use it to find a different life for himself.

The thing was, going through these townhouses and large apartments with Arlene, he could picture it, domestic bliss of a sort. Getting up in the morning, getting the kid off to school, cup of coffee in the kitchen, going to work, coming home to maybe a meal being ready, watching TV in the evening, sitting together on the couch, little picket fence, a kid and a cat, and although one part of him felt warm thinking about this, felt settled, felt destined, another part of him felt the same as he did going through the doors of the Hamilton Detention Centre. His legs were getting ready to run. A fog crept into his head. But the thing about going to jail was he didn't have a choice. Pretty quick his legs would settle down, and somehow, no matter how bad the place was, knowing he had no choice in the matter brought some kind of calm with it. Whereas here, each time they looked in a room and Arlene said something like, "We give it a little paint, it'll be perfect for Wave," he felt his legs twitching, and this thing happening to his head, this fog rolling in.

She'd say, "What's wrong? You don't like it?"

And he'd say, "No. It's okay. I like it."

And she'd say, "You don't like it, we don't have to take it."

And he'd say, "No. It's fine."

Then she'd look at him and say, in a whisper so the owner couldn't hear, "The deal is, you can move out anytime. I just need you to do this so we can get a decent place, me and Wave."

She talked like she'd be getting Wave back the minute she could walk into the Children's Aid office and announce that she'd scored a townhouse with two bedrooms. He knew it wasn't that simple.

The place she liked best, a management company looked after it. The guy showing them the place said they'd want a police check, a criminal background check, they just needed to sign a release for it.

121

Arlene told him they had good references and they were paying cash, first and last. Still need the police check, he told them. Albert found himself feeling relieved. He imagined it showed.

They took a cab back to James Street. She didn't say anything. She sat in the right back corner of the cab not saying anything so loudly he thought he should hop out and get a pair of those industrial ear muffs. They were almost at James when he said, "The second one we looked at. The Polish lady. She liked my name was Wesnicki. Bet we give her first and last she won't ask any questions." Arlene's silence was more deafening. Albert understood this, remembered it from his mother, his sister too. Seemed to be a female thing. They get their minds set on something, they figure the world will fall in place, especially the male world, it'll all come around for them, even if the thing they have in mind is some kind of Cinderella shit.

But Arlene was over it when they got out of the cab and she paid the driver while Albert looked up and down the street. On the stairs, walking ahead of him, she said, "That second place will do for now. We can make it work."

And just before they got to his apartment Albert found himself feeling grateful she'd gotten out of her funk so quickly and returned to making decisions for both of them. Maybe he could get used to it.

The door was open, the lock broken. Albert stepped in ahead of her, looking at a mess. Stuff spilled all over, chair overturned, pillows ripped, kitchen cabinets open, refrigerator door open, mattress cut or ripped, pulled off the bed. At the same time he noticed plain bare wall

122

where his Plasma TV should be he saw Harry lying on the floor. He knelt beside the old man. He was breathing, that smell of acid booze coming from his mouth. Albert couldn't see any new injures, except maybe an abrasion, a welt above his left eye. Otherwise he looked peaceful. Arlene was standing behind Albert, her arms crossed. She said, "I think Jerome found where you live."

Albert said, "Maybe he's just drunk. Maybe he's not hurt."

That's when Harry opened his eyes, the left only partially, and said, "I think they broke my right arm."

Arlene pulled a cell from her purse, began dialling. Albert said, "Tell them someone fell, may have broken his arm. We don't want cops, just an ambulance."

Harry said, "I heard a noise coming from your apartment. Sounded like someone was tearing it apart. I went to see. There was a tall lanky bastard, and this shorter man. The shorter one looked pretty rough, that scabby look you get after a few months of crystal meth. Teeth gone, nose pushed in. The tall one wanted to know where you were. And Arlene. They asked after Arlene as well. Did they smash that bottle you keep, Albert?"

"I'll look," Albert said. Arlene was giving the address to someone on the phone.

Albert found the intact bottle at the back of the cupboard. He took it to Harry, held his head up to drink from it. Arlene began to pick up stuff, tidy it up. Then she brought a kitchen chair over, placed it on its side next to Harry. Albert looked at her. She explained, "The paramedics get here, this is Harry's apartment. He fell from a chair trying to change a light bulb. We hear the crash and find him like this."

"Okay," said Albert. "We leave the door open, they don't notice the broken lock."

Harry said, "Pretty good. Commonest cause of death in my demographic is falling off something you shouldn't be on." He took another sip from the bottle Albert held to his lips. "It was that small mean bastard. Smashed me in the cheek, broke my arm. Figured I'm better off just lying down here and keeping my eyes closed. The tall one wanted to wait, but the short one was hell bent on taking that plasma screen out the back door."

15

Stuff it up the hole in your culture

Jerome was a block behind Billy lugging the big plasma TV. He couldn't see him getting it to the pawn shop on King East or the Stelco parking lot where someone might buy it no questions. Cop drives by and sees a guy looking as bad as Billy lugging a three thousand dollar plasma is gonna stop and ask a few questions. So Jerome kept a half a block to a full block behind Billy, thinking about why it was, no matter how hard he tried to get himself up in the world, he could find himself trailing a meth-head across Hamilton. But if Billy somehow managed to get where he wanted to go and got himself a thousand for it, Jerome was sure gonna get his half. As he followed Billy, Jerome was thinking about that moment in Victoria, when luck intervened, and he suddenly knew he had choices, limited though they were. And again, here, he could let Billy go and wait for Albert, so why was he following Billy? And he thought of that time years ago when a shrink had his mother put him on Ritalin, and then stopped prescribing when they found he was selling it to his friends for a couple of bucks per pill, ground up and ready for snorting.

Billy was holding the plasma screen out in front as he walked, but his arms got tired and so he hoisted it on his shoulder, staggered a little but kept walking. Jerome watched this, figured the odds were slim a cop didn't stop him, or Billy would probably drop the damn thing anyway. There were a few people on the sidewalks but nobody gave

Billy more than a glance. Nobody could figure it a natural thing for a guy dressed like Billy to be lugging a big Plasma up the street but one look at Billy was enough to tell almost anybody that this is not his business.

To Jerome's surprise Billy got all the way to the pawnshop on King East. Jerome waited across the street, standing against the window of an empty storefront, place they used to sell lottery tickets, adult magazines and cigars.

Five, ten minutes standing there, he began to think that when he had had a choice of waiting for Albert to return or following Billy for the possibility of a five hundred dollar payoff, he'd made the wrong decision. For at that moment the plate glass window of the pawnshop exploded into the street, followed by what looked like Albert's now mangled big screen plasma TV.

16

There'll be phantoms

When his mother opened the door to the house on Garland, a light October drizzle starting, Albert said, "Mom, this here's Arlene."

The paramedics had taken Harry away without questioning the circumstances of his fall, or the ownership of the apartment. Arlene made a show of telling Harry, now on the stretcher, his neck and one arm in braces, that they would close up the apartment and look after the cat while he's in hospital. She explained to Albert later that it was details like looking after a cat that always sold the lie. "But there is no cat." Said Albert.

"There you go," she said.

He threw some clothes in a bag, took his tooth brush and razor, his bag of toiletries, and they locked up, going down the back stairs in case Jerome was watching the apartment entrance. He asked if she had a place to go, and she said no, but she was going to buy some clothes first. He realized he knew little about her. "Do you have any family?" he asked, as she rummaged through the bins and racks of Morgenstern, just a couple of blocks up from his apartment.

She didn't stop or turn to him when she answered, "None that I'm talking to."

As she paid, and then walked out with her bags, and waited for a cab, she seemed to be, as always, a step ahead of him. When they had gotten into the cab, and he had given the address of his mother's house,

127

and then turned to her to explain, he had the distinct feeling that she already knew the address, knew who lived there, and knew he would take her there. And Albert found himself anxious, feeling like a schoolboy taking a very unacceptable girl home to meet the family. He had no idea how his mother would react.

What his mother did was, she let her eyes pass slowly across Arlene standing just to the side and slightly behind Albert, then fixed on Albert and said, "I'm not giving you any money."

Albert said, "I don't need any money. Not this time. Can we come in and have a coffee, you know, talk?"

She said, "And after that it'll get around to money. It always does."

"No. I swear to God. Not this time. But we are in a bit of trouble."

Mrs. Wesnicki glanced at Arlene's taught midriff, making the obvious assumption. She said, "All right. Come in. I'll make a fresh pot."

They sat at the kitchen table in silence while his mother busied herself with the coffee, brought cream and sugar to the table. Arlene put her bags beside her chair and sat stiffly, hands crossed on her lap, as if back in parochial school. Albert looked at the kitchen through Arlene's eyes. His mother had the same stove and refrigerator, the same set of cutting knives on the same counter, trivets, toaster, blender, the same frilly curtain, the window sill and corner cabinet filled with small glass ornaments. His mother was a woman who distracted herself with small inexpensive pleasures, whose taste leaned towards sweet. A

128

portrait of the last pope, the Polish one, still hung over the kitchen table, looking upon them with those kind but knowing eyes. Some out-of-date schedules were still attached to the refrigerator and one piece each of Albert's and his sister's juvenile art, somehow still fresh and innocent. Red, blue, green, and yellow, the sun a circle with rays, the sky a line of blue above, the small house with oversized windows, stick figures, a dog in the corner. There was only one stick figure in Albert's drawing, frontal view, standing beside the house, with a big grin on his round face and an oversized gun in his hand. The whole family was featured in his sister's drawing, with baby Albert mostly head, and his father off in the corner.

His mother poured the newly dripped coffee, put Carnation condensed milk in her own. Arlene asked if she could try that as well. His mother said sure, and gave her the can. With three sugars and a dollop of Carnation, Arlene pronounced it pretty good. Mrs. Wesnicki said, "There you go, Albert. I'm not the only one likes it this way." And then to Arlene, "He thinks it's very unsophisticated, putting sweet canned milk in coffee." Arlene smiled and Mrs. Wesnicki got right to the point. "Albert hasn't got you pregnant, has he?"

"Mom, Jesus." Said Albert.

Arlene said, "No, I'm not pregnant, Mrs. Wesnicki." And then she explained for both of them why they were here. Albert sat quietly listening to Arlene's version of events into which she poured a lot of detail while merely altering Jerome's motive. Albert owed him money from a year ago when Albert was using drugs, and Jerome just recently found where he was living. Which was her fault, really, because she'd moved in with Albert a month ago and Jerome had tracked her down. He demanded his money and Albert gave him his big screen TV but he wanted more, like a hundred percent interest, and he trashed the place and said he'd be back. So they were temporarily without a place to live but they'd looked at a nice duplex over on Warren.

His mother said, "You've been living together for a month and my son didn't tell me?"

"He doesn't make commitments easily, Mrs. Wesnicki."

"Please call me Gloria," his mother said, and then Albert found himself becoming invisible, as these two women, Arlene and Gloria, talked and talked. Very quickly Gloria learned (and Albert indirectly) that Arlene was 24. She grew up in a large catholic family, five children, went to St. Thomas More Secondary, got pregnant at 17, still managed to finish her grade twelve, but her father put her out. She's been on her own ever since, trying to raise her baby. Now six. Wave. "What a beautiful name," Gloria said. And Arlene told of getting into a bad relationship, of using drugs, of Children's Aid apprehending Wave, but how she's getting her life back together now and how she's learned the only important thing in her life is Wave and how she's made a commitment to Jesus to do whatever it takes to go straight and get Wave back and how when she gets a chance she wants to go to College to become a teacher.

If there hadn't been much riding on this conversation, Albert was sure he would have acted upon his impulse to leap from his chair, fling his arms in the air and shout, "Hallelujah, praise Jesus. Praise the Lord."

130

His mother, to Albert's surprise, said, "Everybody makes mistakes, Sweetie, and everybody deserves a second chance."

Albert, up looking for biscuits or something else edible in the cupboards above the counter, said, without looking at them, "This second chance stuff. That hold for your son as well?"

His mother, Gloria, said, not taking her eyes off Arlene, "I believe, by now, you're up to chance seven or eight."

Albert sat with a box of Peak Freans, made a face and munched. He resisted stating his almost habitual litany of excuses, reasons, newly discovered insights and promises. The last time he had stood before a judge and the judge, in response to his attorney's plea for probation and another chance, had asked, "When did you realize you had a drug problem, Mr. Wesnicki?" Albert had answered, with his practiced tone of contrition, "Just now, your honour." And the judge had laughed and given him nine months less double time served, which came out to five months. Five months clean and sober to think about his brand new discovery. And a guy like Albert didn't get drugs in jail. He knew no one who would deliver them, and he had nothing he wanted to sell. So he got straight, did his time, and met Jerome.

While he munched on these biscuits that always tasted better dipped in sweet coffee, Gloria and Arlene talked like old friends. Two women who had seen hard times and been wronged by men. Any minute now, the baby pictures would come out. The other thing he noticed was absolutely no mention of his father, as if Gloria had conceived and raised Albert and his sister on her own. He didn't think his mother was avoiding this topic on account of his father's suicide, but simply because, in the lives and futures of these women, men were irrelevant. At best, a means to an end.

Gloria finally asked them to stay for dinner, though she didn't have much, and while Arlene helped her in the kitchen, Albert retired to the living room to watch Judge Judy. He first stuck his head in the refrigerator and Gloria pointed out he wouldn't find any beer in there. There'd been no alcohol in the house since his father died. He took a glass of juice instead. The television hadn't been changed, the furniture the same, the same lamps and reproductions on the walls, the same family pictures on the mantelpiece. Albert settled into the chair that had been his father's for years, put down in the basement when the new leather La Z Boy was purchased, and brought back up after the ruined chair was taken to the dump. Not right away, maybe a month later, to fill the void. These people, Judge Judy's people, were always trying to heal the holes in their hearts through lawsuits. Always in-laws, cousins, ex-lovers, one of them usually just out of jail, and Judge Judy rolling her eyes, throwing up her hands and saying, "How did I know that?" Albert understood he liked the show because it featured a whole bunch of people who made even more stupid decisions than he did.

Supper was meat pies, creamed corn, hash browns from a bag, and lots of ketchup. "You want perogies, you have to give me notice," his mother said.

After dinner his mother told them they could stay, with Arlene in Christine's room. She'd gotten rid of the bed and made it into her computer room, her internet room, but she had a nice pull out couch, she explained. She'd hardly touched Albert's old room, expecting to see him back before his sister, but lord knows, Christine might be coming home as well, with two grandchildren, if she doesn't patch things up with her husband. She didn't explain the separate rooms; the image of the Pope over the kitchen table was enough.

They took turns in the bathroom and then Albert entered his old bedroom for the first time in, he wasn't sure, about four years. Gloria had cleaned it out, with the exception of the original bed, one chair, and a desk in the corner upon which sat his three hockey trophies, all earned before he turned fifteen and discovered, in this order, beer, marijuana, hash, rum and coke, vodka shots, girls, Ecstacy, Cocaine, and Crystal meth.

He lay on the same mattress he had slept on for as long as he could remember, on which he'd had chicken pox and whooping cough as a kid, and under which he'd stored his Penthouse magazines, and Hustler, and on which he'd masturbated quietly those many nights, with a chair against the door in case his mother or sister should decide to visit at that moment, and on which he'd lain with spinning head and stomach in his mouth after sneaking back in before dawn. He remembered the one time he made it, maybe four in the morning, got past his parents' room successfully, lay down on his bed, watched the ceiling turn in on itself, felt the nausea well up, figured he'd never make it to the bathroom, went for the window instead, pulled it open, stuck his head out, and vomited down the side of the house. Feeling better and thinking he'd gotten away with it again, he slept. But his bedroom was on the second floor, and evidence of his over indulgence was spattered down the side of the house from his window to the cellar.

This was a strange feeling he had, trying to put his finger on it. Arlene in the next room, his mother in the master bedroom downstairs, or on the couch in the living room, childhood memories colliding with both guilt and anticipation, the boy inside him colliding with his homelessness, his failures, and still, lying there, aware he had an erection. He could really use a hit of something about now.

She entered the room so quietly she had slipped under the covers before he fully realized. "Shhh," they told one another in unison. After kissing his lips, his chest, she pulled him on top of her, and said, "I want you inside me."

Afterward, after the hushed, stolen, cautious coupling, with Arlene lying in the crook of his arm, Albert relaxed into the safety, the security of this moment's illusion.

17

Don't like children anyhow

At the Children's Services Office on Upper James, Arlene, now sans lip and tongue ring, told Penny she had a new address, that she'd moved in with the mother of a friend while she looked for an affordable apartment. "A nice woman," she said. "A widow, very old fashioned."

She was there for a one-hour visit, a one-hour supervised visit with Wave, watched by Penny, her new worker. Albert had offered to come with her and she had turned him down. It was bad enough on her own, feeling the humiliation, the discomfort, the utter shame of being watched and judged on how she, as they would call it, interacted, with her own daughter, without his eyes upon her as well. Besides, as an ex-con drug dealing boyfriend, he would not help her case. They would judge him quickly and harshly, even if he were on his best behaviour. First he would have to learn to say, with complete sincerity, "Yes ma'am, no ma'am", and do the twelve step.

Penny was about forty, and had children of her own, which was a great improvement after the first two workers assigned to her case, who had been fresh out of school, full of text book ideas about children, with no real experience. They had sent her to parenting classes, anger management classes, when the real problem had been the men in her life. Which was, she had to admit, her problem really. And the drugs. She had told Penny she had been too young, just too young to have a kid on her own, but now she was ready. Penny seemed to understand

135

this, had a little sympathy. Wave was on a six-month supervision order, which would become permanent if she didn't turn this around pretty quick. I'm trying honey, I'm trying, she said to herself.

Penny, glasses attached to a lace looped behind her neck, brown hair short and bobbed, a sensible suit, placed herself in a chair in the corner of the observation room, and Arlene sat in the other corner awaiting the delivery of Wave. As she waited, Arlene had to resist allowing her anxiety to turn into anger, anger at Penny putting her through this, anger at the foster mother who was always late delivering Wave, anger at the impossibility of acting in any remotely natural fashion with her daughter, with Penny watching and sometimes making notes. And Goddamit, what they called 'inappropriate', one of their favourite words, along with 'concerns', fell well within the boundaries of what she understood, in her own experience, to be simple normal human behaviour. Maybe not perfect human behaviour, but pretty common nonetheless.

On one visit she had been told, afterwards, that they had concerns about her inappropriate statements of affection, which, she imagined, referred to a moment when she clutched Wave to herself, tickled her, and said, "I just love you so much I could eat you up." And the time they gave her shit for promising something she could not control. "I just told her she'd be back with me soon. We'd be a team again. That's all." That's for a judge to decide, they told her. And 'team' is not an appropriate term for a mother-daughter relationship. They have concerns about her parenting skills. They always have fucking concerns.

136

The door opened and Wave came in, shyly, glancing back at someone out of sight saying, "Go on, dear." For a moment she stood there, first glancing at Penny, and then looking down but watching Arlene out of the corner of her eye. Arlene wished with all her might that Wave would rush forward, arms outstretched, shouting "Mommy." And then she could catch her in her own arms and hug her and then smile at observant Penny, who was this very minute jotting something in her note book. Something like, "The child appears hesitant in mother's presence."

And what child wouldn't be hesitant? What child ever gives herself freely to someone whom she knows will abandon her again in sixty short minutes? Arlene held her breath. She didn't want to go to Wave. She was pretty sure that would generate a note that read something like, "Child hesitant. Mother forces herself upon child.". Wave was wearing little jeans with flower appliqués, her blonde hair tied in a bow to one side. She had a face most men would see as angelic, but which might concern some mothers as being a little pale, perhaps undernourished. A petite nose. A tiny chin. Arlene stifled a tear, leaned forward and said, "Hello, Sweetie."

18

When they said repent

Sam said, "I want you to know I did not mention your hypothetical question to anyone."

"Why would you?" Albert asked. She was on time today, ushered him into her office efficiently.

"Because, what you were asking about sounded suspiciously like a recent situation over on Wentworth. A house fire, and they find a known drug dealer inside dead from a gunshot."

Albert put on his most charming smile. "And you didn't tell anybody because?"

When she said nothing, Albert added, "Trust building, huh? Developing rapport with your client."

She was on the other side of the desk dressed in a small jacket over a simple top that revealed just a hint. He wasn't sure it was a plus or a minus having an attractive woman as his probation officer, women being more complicated than men. With a male PO he could just assume he did not have a friend, a supporter. The guy might do his best for his boys, but he'd breach you blink of an eye. Unless it would mean a lot of work and the breach was so minor a judge would throw it out and give him shit. But a woman, this woman anyway, could look so sympathetic, so interested, he might start believing he could tell her anything. And he had the feeling if he lied to her she'd take it personally. Besides, his natural instinct, when confronted by an attractive woman, was to flirt, or to put on his best "I'm available" face. He figured it was biological. But neither approach was wise with your PO. And now she was telling him, "Albert, I think you can make it this time. I'm going to ride your ass because I'm optimistic. You're smart. You're too smart to continue the shit you've been in. And maybe you're maturing a little. I've got you for another eighteen months. You don't fuck me over I'll be in your corner all the way. So tell me why you've moved back in with your momma?"

Albert recognized the "ride your ass" and "fuck me over" as phrases she'd borrowed from her male colleagues. They didn't come natural to her. But he found himself wanting to please her, and get inside her pants too, of course, but that last impulse gave him a twinge of guilt with the smell of Arlene still upon him. He told Sam why he moved back with his momma, using Arlene's version of events, without Arlene in the story. He couldn't mention Arlene yet, until he was sure she wasn't on some cop list or something, and Sam would breach him for 'associating'.

After his story, which she seemed to buy, (but then again, who can tell with a woman?), she asked about his father. He said, "You know. It's right there in your records. He worked the steel mills all his life, after getting here from Poland his late teens or something, you know, when it was still Communist. And then he killed himself. All there is to it."

She said, "You ever think about that? What it was like for him at your age?"

139

And Albert knew he'd be here a while today, talking, trying not to tell her too much, Sam getting more from him than he wanted to give. He figured she'd taken some workshop lately, some counselling bullshit. Post Traumatic Stress was in these days, explaining why he turned to drugs and criminal behaviour, like it could never be just the natural thing to do, but who the fuck really knows. Or maybe that line of questioning was the Empathy Thing. See if he could relate to someone else's pain and hardship. Anyway, he'd have to indulge her, answer her questions, let her feel she was earning her keep, doing her job.

Almost an hour later, after he'd told her some of the truth, given a little of himself, at least as much as he knew of himself, and after she, he had to admit, made him think a little about his dad in terms other than "a hard-working, hard-drinking, loser" she said, suddenly all business, the sympathetic look gone from her face, "Okay. Enough for today. I'll see you in two weeks, same time, same place. Leave a sample on your way out. And Albert, treat your mother good. She's been through a lot."

19

My secret room, my secret life

They were having breakfast together, the family. His mother had made poached eggs, toast, and set the table with jams, butter, and cheeses. And coffee of course, with canned milk. "Years ago," she conceded, "In a good restaurant, like a CP hotel, they'd bring coffee in one silver jug and hot milk in the other, and pour them at the same time. Into a proper cup and saucer. Now if someone were to do that for me today, that's the way I'd take it. Proper café au lait."

"You can get that at Starbucks if you want." He told her, a mouth full of poached egg and toast.

"What, with two silver jugs, a nice cup, and a handsome man pouring?"

"Not exactly."

"And at three fifty a mug I'll stick to my Tim Hortons, thank you very much."

"You ought to open your own coffee shop," he told her. "You can turn everybody onto canned milk with their coffee. We can call it Café au Carnation. Or Caffe con Carnationi. Or, I got it, Café incarnation."

She said, "Go ahead, make fun. Soon I'll be charging you room and board."

Arlene said, "Well, my parents used to drink, I remember now, instant coffee. A spoon of Nescafe and boiling water, three sugars."

141

"It was the Second World War," his mother said. "Killed a lot of people, but it also ruined food in North America. That's where instant and processed food comes from. It was all about convenience."

Albert's eyebrows were raised, looking at her, over his coffee con Carnation.

She said, as explanation, "I read a lot these days, now there's just me in this house."

He was noticing things. The cloth napkins on the table, the silo-shaped white porcelain salt and pepper shakers, the sugar bowl, the one kitchen window with it's flowered curtain and knickknacks, the old light fixture in the middle of the ceiling, his mother's hair speckled grey, cut short, her sweater, the kitchen chairs, three functional, one with broken rung waiting to be repaired, the kitchen cabinets with old crescent pulls. He was sure nothing had been changed since he last lived here and yet he was seeing everything for the first time, even his mother, her shade of lipstick, reading glasses always at the ready, her sad and tired eyes, the friendly and easy way she talked to Arlene. He wasn't sure if it had been simple adolescent inattention before, or the fact he was usually either stoned, or thinking about getting stoned.

Gloria said, "Your friend Kyle. From some years ago. The one you used to get in trouble with."

He waited for it, expecting something like, "I hope you're not associating with him again. I never liked that boy."

Instead she said, "I think he died."

He said, "What?"

"It's in the paper this morning. The obituaries."

142

"You read the obituaries?"

She ignored his question, went on, "If it's the same Kyle Hill. Survived by his mother Francine, his step-father Donald, two sisters, one niece, and I think a grandmother."

Albert said, "That's his last name. I can't think of his mother's name but his step-father was Donald. Used to call him Donald Chump. And two younger sisters. Was it really in the obituaries?"

"That's what I just said."

"Holy shit. I haven't seen him for a couple of years. Not since.....". He thought about that afternoon he lay down in the middle of Bay Street outside the crack house, and the night they were busted at the Zanzibar. "How did he die? Did it say?"

"It just said 'suddenly', and no mention of a viewing or a funeral, which means, at that age, either suicide or a violent death. You know what I think: it was probably a drug overdose. The only shooting recently was that Jamaican over on Wentworth."

Trying to skip past this trend in the conversation, Albert said, "Maybe he signed up, you know, was over in Afghanistan, fighting the Taliban."

"Albert, if he'd been a soldier fighting for his country, it would have been front page news. There'd be a big article about it."

"I guess. You read it this morning, huh?"

"The paper's over there. Read it yourself, you don't take my word for it. You knew him since when, the seventh grade?"

Not ready to digest this news, Albert said, "Remember you tried to get me to sign up, a few years back?"

143

She said, "I remember. I thought it might straighten you out. And there was no war going on at the time. Not one Canada was in, anyway. You'd have a trade by now, or a college education."

"Or I'd be in Afghanistan being shot at by some toothless guy doesn't believe women should be taught to read." But in his mind he was picturing Kyle, Kyle with the big laugh, Kyle who pulled him off the street that day, Kyle who was ready to try anything, Kyle and him popping E's at a Rave in Toronto, Kyle strung out on Meth, Kyle selling Oxycontins to buy his Meth, getting them from a doc on Barton, Kyle who always had big plans, Kyle showing him room service, ordering his drugs from Pakistan off the internet, Kyle probably re-upping once to often, mixing shit. They were the same age, give or take a month or two. Compulsively he took another slice of toast and put a good layer of peanut butter on it. "What an asshole," he said.

"Who?" asked his mother.

"Kyle."

"That's no way to speak of the dead."

"You know what I mean. Jesus. Stupid bugger." Kyle who had pulled him off the street. Kyle for whom he'd done nothing. Just watched him get deeper and deeper into it.

His mother said, "Anyone want more coffee au Carnation?"

Arlene held out her mug, but Albert, preoccupied, got up and began clearing the dishes, taking them to the sink, then opening the dishwasher and putting them in.

His mother watched this. Then she turned to Arlene, while she poured the coffee, and said, "I don't believe my eyes. Are you seeing what I'm seeing?"

20

Give me back the Berlin wall

The General Hospital had grown to the edges of Barton Street, with a new entrance facing the corner on Victoria. Barton was a street enlivened over the years by waves of immigrants come to work the steel mills, fabrication plants, Westinghouse, General Electric, Proctor and Gamble, Stelco, Dofasco, even Studebaker, and parts for GM, rail cars, tankers, motors, trestles, bridges, toothpaste and Listerine. Dofasco was still thriving but now owned by Germans or Russians, maybe Indians, he couldn't remember which. Stelco had slipped quietly into receivership; the rest were long gone, leaving behind acres of crumbling buildings and what they were calling brown space between Barton and the lake, dotted with small worn houses, piles of scrap, and empty sheds.

Some of the damage had been done, he knew, by the underside of prosperity and the growing expectations of next generations, like himself. Production fled to lands with cheaper labour, leaving decay, and civic leaders stymied, wishing the industry back. The storefronts on Barton changed frequently, new signs scribbled over old, and then gone again. Used Appliances, variety stores, junk stores, cigarettes and Lotto tickets, liquidation centres, empty windows. No sign of fresh paint on any of them. A couple of small bars, one in the old Bank of Montreal building, its name still visible in the stone mantle above the entrance, and the strip joint that had acquired a new name but would always be known as Hanrahans, featuring, since the fall of the Soviet Empire, Russian girls.

Like an archaeological site, remnants of each era could be found in the layers of mill dust coating every surface. Conical spires of a Hungarian Church, St. Stephens, a Serbian Club, a Croatian Centre, and a decorated shop selling Polish sausage and perogies. The Italians dominated once, but all they left behind when they moved to the west of James and the suburbs was a funeral parlour and an old Trattoria. Then Portuguese, and now Jamaicans and Vietnamese, selling from kitchens assembled quickly in dirty storefronts: Churrasquiera, Roti, Jerk Chicken, Spring rolls, Noodles. A large brick elementary school transformed into a neighbourhood multicultural centre. The old Barton Gaol had grown into the Hamilton Wentworth Detention Centre and then the Hamilton Detention Centre, of which he was now all too familiar. It sat between a Dunkin' Donuts parking lot and an empty nineteenth century workhouse, and across from The Crowbar Café, which must have been named, he often thought, when the owner was high on something.

For several blocks the city had tried, in an act of appeasement, indented curbs, trees, flowers, and a centre strip of planters. It quickly absorbed the decaying patina of the rest of the neighbourhood.

Albert found himself thinking about these things, now that he was no longer either stoned or on the hustle, as he and Arlene entered the General Hospital to visit another decaying relic, Harry. Arlene had called the hospital and found that Harry McCracken was still on the Orthopedic ward, but not being able to say, or prove, that she was

147

immediate family, she acquired no other information. It was now November, but still warm, and three days since the paramedics took Harry away.

On the Orthopedic floor they enquired of his room number and were once again asked if they were immediate family. Albert watched as Arlene effortlessly went into her act, telling the nurse that Harry was her grandfather, that his son lived in Vancouver, and his daughter, her mother, was out of the country on business and couldn't get back. The nurse, a plump motherly type, said they'd been trying to reach a next of kin, that Harry in his few lucid moments had mentioned a daughter.

"That must be my mother." Arlene interjected.

But we don't have a phone number, the nurse continued. The social worker was looking into it because they were pretty sure it was time for Harry to go into Long Term Care. "I'm afraid he's really quite demented, my dear," she said to Arlene.

"Are you sure we're talking about the same Harry?" asked Albert.

"You can visit," said the nurse, ignoring Albert. "But he might not even recognize you. The doctor has ordered an MRI to be on the safe side, but he's pretty sure it's Alzheimer's."

When Arlene had called herself the granddaughter of Harry, Albert had wondered if Harry was old enough for a granddaughter over, say, ten or eleven. But when they saw Harry, he realized that would pose no difficulties, for Harry had aged ten years in his hospital gown, prone on the bed, tied down with what Albert had unfortunately come to know were called four point leathers: padded leather cuffs on each wrist and ankle, tethered to the bed railings. In Harry's case that would be three point leathers, because his right arm was locked in a cast from shoulder to wrist, the whole fixed to a pulley above the bed. A man in a similar contraption of cast and pulleys lay on the other bed, close to the window, his plaster arm concealing his face.

"Holy shit," said Albert, before he could stop himself. "What the frig have they done to you?"

The nurse, who had followed them into the room, quickly explained, "It's for his own good. If we didn't tie him down he'd be breaking another bone or two. And he hit one of the aides with that cast. The doctor has him heavily sedated as well."

Albert stepped closer, and saw Harry's mouth moving, his eyelids twitching, his dank hair and beard, the tremor in his fingers despite the leathers. He was mouthing words, some audible, some not. Arlene stepped to the foot of the bed and from that position she could see the face of the second patient and he, unfortunately, could see hers.

And the second man began shouting. "You." He said. "You bitch, you whore. Don't let them near me. Don't let them near me." He repeated his words, again and again, with increasing volume, punctuated by yelps of pain as he struggled to sit upright and get in position to run.

Albert said, "Holy fucking shit. It's the Raincoat Guy."

Harry's jumble of words became audible, then louder, in volume echoing the Raincoat Guy, in snatches of rhyme and inconsequential observation. "You can see it in the stars. And the twinkle of a whore when Christmas comes. There's just not that many

149

any more. Rum a tum tum." And then just words, as if a thesaurus in his head had sprung a leak.

"I think the visit is over," said the nurse, visibly confused.

"Harry. It's me. Albert. Harry. Look at me."

The nurse rushed from the room as the Raincoat Guy, Charley, got himself to a sitting position, flailed with the wires and pulleys, screaming now, just wailing. Albert was still trying to get Harry to focus.

Arlene said, "Come on, Albert. We can't do anything here." She pulled at his arm and they left together, followed by Harry's stream of dislocated words, and Charley's howls of pain. In the corridor they passed an old security guard walking slowly in the direction of Harry's room.

At the nursing station, the plump nurse put the phone down, turned to them, a little breathless. "Do you know that other man?"

"No. Not at all." Said Arlene.

"He was found beaten up. Apparently he had no identification. You certainly set him off."

The intercom over their heads came to life and announced, "Code White", and Harry's room number. The noise from the end of the corridor was already subsiding when a small group of determined men and women in scrubs and white jackets rushed past. The nurse went on, "He wouldn't tell the police anything about who beat him up. There's an awful lot of that happening these days."

But Albert was determined to talk about Harry. He said, "Look. I don't think he's senile. He's probably in DT's."

"The homeless man?"

"No. Harry. Arlene's grandfather."

"You think he's in DT's?"

"Yes. It's probably three, four days since he's had a drink."

"You're saying he's an alcoholic."

"Yes. And this is probably withdrawal. Not Alzheimer's. He was good before. More than good."

"I'm sure the doctor would have considered that."

"Look. I'm telling you. It's alcohol. Not Alzheimer's. He needs treatment for it." Albert could see the nurse was struggling with this, irritated, her orderly day already upset.

She composed herself and said, in her best placating voice, "I'll mention your concerns to the MRP."

"The MRP?"

"In cases like your grandfather's, with multiple problems such as a fractured elbow, and dementia, several teams are involved. One doctor is designated the MRP, the Most Responsible Physician. That would be Doctor Chan for your grandfather."

"And when would you mention this to the MRP?"

"When he does his rounds later today."

"That may be too late," said Albert. "First there's confusion, then hallucinations, then this talking nonsense, and then seizures, and then everything goes out of whack, and people die in DT's."

"I'm sure the doctor will look into it."

"You're not listening to me, are you?"

Arlene said, "This won't get us anywhere, Albert. Let's get out of here."

The small group of whites and scrubs were coming back from their duties on the front lines of Harry's room. Emboldened, the nurse said to the space between Albert and Arlene, "I'm sure you've done enough damage for one day."

That's when Arlene lost it. The word "concerns" had kindled the fire, and she knew her anger rightfully belonged with Children's Services, but she turned on the hapless nurse, "Listen you fat cunt. You just make sure you tell your Dr. Chan exactly what my husband said."

They didn't speak on the way out, with Arlene's gaze fixed, and Albert following, not sure he was more surprised by her outburst or the word, "husband".

Outside, when she stopped to take a breath, she asked him, "How do you know that stuff, about DT's I mean? Or were you just making it up?"

"What was that 'husband' shit?" he asked in turn.

In the taxi, going back to his mother's, he told her, when she had asked a second time. "My uncle. My father's older brother. They came out together. I used to talk to him, a lot more than my father. They got out of Poland not long before the union strikes. Ended up in some DP camp together. They wanted to go to Australia, meet some kangaroos. Seriously, that's what he told me. They'd seen pictures of all that sun, beaches and kangaroos. That's where they wanted to go. But Australia had its quota of Polacks or something, and Canada was next on the list. There was still lots of work in Hamilton back then, and the rest is history."

"The DT's. Remember?"

"Well, that's the point. My Uncle. He was quite a boozer. I think he put Vodka on his corn flakes in the morning. He never married, so he was around a lot in those days, came for dinner most weekends. I dunno. I was about fifteen, he gets Multiple Myeloma, I think they called it, in his back. His English was never very good. They put him in hospital 'cause of the pain. And then five days later he has a seizure and dies. Just like that. The doctors told my father the tumour must have spread to his brain and caused the seizure. They said it was a blessing he went so fast. My father said that was all bullshit. He'd been barred from visiting because he'd taken his brother a bottle of Vodka. They confiscated it, the pricks. He changed after that, I think. He always drank but he usually got funny, harmless anyway, or he'd come home and sleep it off. But after my uncle died he'd get, you know, maudlin, and tell the story over and over, the next few years. So I heard it a hundred times. And twice at Christmas. A drunk goes into the hospital and doesn't tell them how much he drinks, pretty soon he's going cold turkey, on top of whatever else is happening, and then he gets fucked. They don't know shit. That's why I keep a bottle for Harry at all times. That's how they used to treat DT's, you know. Get the alcohol levels back up. Now they give you anti-seizure drugs, tranquillizers, and minerals and shit. We're gonna have to get Harry out of there before he has a seizure and croaks."

"We can't take him home with the cast and pulley and stuff. And Jerome still looking for us."

"Then I'll have to take him some medicine myself, as soon as that fat bitch goes off duty."

So Albert took medicine to Harry each evening the next four days. He'd carry the bottle in his jacket pocket, go up the elevator with the other relatives and friends visiting between seven and nine, get off on the orthopaedic floor, head the opposite way if he saw alert staff at the nursing station, then wait for the moment they had their heads buried in charts, and walk quietly past.

In Harry's room, the second bed was empty now. It held Albert's attention for a second, somehow reminding him of the death of his uncle and of the inevitability of tragedy. It appeared to be waiting patiently for the next person to stray across the double line. But he imagined Charley had been simply moved to another room so the two old crocks couldn't set one another off.

There was no recognition in Harry's eyes the first two nights; he muttered softly and incoherently to himself. An IV was attached to his good arm and Albert hoped the fat nurse had actually spoken to the MRP who might not be fresh out of school, and who might have put some replacement chemicals in the saline solution. Albert found the button that raised the head of the bed and simply put the lip of his bottle on Harry's lower lip. Harry's muttering stopped. He licked at the edge. He took the bottle the way a baby might, or a dog. Albert poured a

154

spoonful or two in Harry's mouth, watched him swallow, and poured some more.

He tended to Harry carefully, pleased he wasn't causing coughing or choking. Those first two nights he wasn't sure Harry understood what was happening; his lapping at the liquid might be instinct. When Harry's eyes appeared to stop their wandering, their inward searching, and focus briefly on first the bottle, and then Albert's face, they betrayed no glimmer of recognition, no sign of certainty, only confusion, questioning. But on the third night, with Albert's thumb on the button that raised the head of the bed, his other hand pulling the bottle from his pocket, Harry said, "Albert." It wasn't a question. It was a truncated statement. And later, after the administration of a good six ounces of medicine, Harry said, simply, "Thank you."

The next few nights, when Albert visited, he found that Harry had already raised the head of the bed in anticipation, and his cast had been changed to one that looked smaller and lighter, simply held in a sling around his neck. He told Albert that Dr. Chan had found his recovery quite amazing, that he would have to change his diagnosis, and that, if he had someone to look after him while he was still in a cast, and a little weak, he could go home in a day or two. You could let my daughter know I'm here, he told Albert, and started to give him the phone number, but couldn't quite remember it. "Damn," he said. "It's written somewhere, but the nurses have my wallet. You could ask at the desk." Albert explained he probably shouldn't ask at the desk, that his visits were on the sly. Harry looked puzzled and Albert told him of the first visit with Arlene. Harry smiled and said, "Too bad you didn't have a tape recorder. That might have been the best stuff I've produced in years."

Albert said, "While you're in here, you might get them to give you a shave, trim your beard up a little."

"More importantly," said Harry. "Bring me something to read. And some drug store reading glasses, number two focus. Get them at one of those discount places. Shouldn't be more than five bucks."

"Sure. What would you like to read?"

"Did I say 'read'? I meant write. Bring me something with which to write. A decent pen and a notebook or two. I'll pay for it later."

Albert said, "Your right arm is in a cast, remember?"

"I'll write with my left," said Harry. "And Albert…"

"What?"

"Nothing. Just watch out for that bastard who broke my arm, that's all."

Albert said, "I will. We're staying with my mother for now."

He had put the bottle back in his pocket and was on his feet ready to leave when Harry said, "You know, Albert, you're really a nice young man."

Albert felt himself blushing, and pleased by Harry's words, which was why he had to answer, as he moved to the door, "Ah, fuck off."

21

Lie beside me baby, that's an order

That night when she slipped into his room, he decided it was time to get a few things straight. He wasn't sure why he decided this night was a good night to talk. His timing, he knew, was not always reliable. Why could he not accept this woman as she appeared to be at this moment? They would make love; they would fuck; she was playful, and sweet; she was clear about her needs. What more could any man want? Jesus. But it troubled him. She was Dervon's whore when he first met her, and then a willing partner of Jerome, and then he still didn't know if she'd set the thing up with Charley, and then he finds she's got a history and a kid named Wave. Said she'd been kicking to get her daughter back, but shit. What was she doing shacked up with a Jamaican drug dealer if she was trying to kick? On the other hand, he hadn't seen her use since they met.

He was unresponsive when she crawled into his bed. She read this immediately and said, "What's wrong?"

And he said, despite having made the decision that tonight was the night to get a few things straight, "Nothing."

"Bullshit." She said. "Something's on your mind. Spit it out."

He rolled on his back, not looking at her. He said, "Now don't get me wrong. It's just I don't know who you are. That's all."

"You know who I am. It's something else, isn't it?"

157

"No. That's it." He rolled to look at her. "You lost your kid on account of drugs. I meet you, you're living with this black guy, a dealer. And now you're mother of the fucking year."

"It's the black guy thing, isn't it?"

"No. White. Purple, Black. Who gives a shit? It's all the rest."

"No it's not. You don't care I'm a good mother or bad mother, whether I'm using or not. It's the black thing. I was fucking a black guy. That's what's got you in a twist."

"Okay. So tell me why you were trying to get straight, you'd live with a Jamaican dealer?"

"I needed money. To get my own place. I figured…besides, you know what? The Children's Services didn't know he was a dealer, just I start showing up with a well dressed black guy, my new boyfriend. He didn't have a record. They don't question it."

"I sure as hell would."

"Well they don't. They can't assume a well dressed black guy is a dealer."

"If he ain't a baseball player."

"That's the point. They'd be in shit they start profiling or something. I show up with you, they can ask straight out: Is this guy using or dealing drugs? I show up with Dervon they can't ask shit. Besides, he was polite, had his grade twelve."

"So why'd you want out of that?"

"He was controlling me. Had me on a fucking allowance. And I could see the Children's Services weren't going to ask the questions direct, but they knew this wasn't the Waltons."

"But you fucked him. Was he good?" The moment Albert asked that question and heard his churlish tone of voice, he knew he was in trouble.

"Fuck you." She said. "Just fuck you." And she left his bed, walked from the room and went back to his sister's room.

22

I wondered what they meant

Jerome decided (there again, he actually decided) to stay and watch this thing unfold. Then again, maybe he didn't decide. There was nothing else catching his immediate attention about now. Across the street, with glass and electronics lying on the sidewalk, a big bald guy in a wheelchair going east pulled up short. And then motored on by as if this was not an unusual occurrence. A couple of kids, hanging out at the homeless Christian youth drop-in place up the street, sauntered closer, staying on Jerome's side of King. He could smell that sweet musty promise of marijuana wafting off them. A guy on a bicycle covered with all sorts of weird shit, mostly hubcaps, a couple of signs about Jesus, the guy dressed in wool coat and a toque with ear flaps, pulled up to the mess on the sidewalk, ignored the shouting coming from inside the store, and began looking through the debris, looking for anything still worth a buck.

Then almost the same time as two cop cars pulled in blocking traffic, bubble lights going, Billy come running out of the pawn shop, heading east hell bent for leather. One of the cops saw Billy, but they took their time getting out, conferring a little, sizing the place up. One female cop, blonde hair pulled up under her cap, tugs on her belt riding high on her hips, one tall black guy, model good looks, aware of it, two shorter white guys, broad shoulders. One of the white guys gets the job

160

of going after Billy, the other three step over the glass and go in the pawn shop.

The cops scanned up, down, across the street before going in and Jerome instinctively shrunk against the empty storefront. But a few more people had gathered now, looked like a junky taking a break from his panhandling, and a couple young guys from the sex shop two doors up, a couple of teen girls all tarted up, black and pink hair, trying their best to look casual. And traffic was stopped now, blocking King and most of the view across the street.

Jerome sees Billy a block away head into the food store, Denningers, foods of the world, the one classy store on this street hadn't moved to the suburbs. The cop on foot sees him too, and stops to talk on his two-way. Then, almost like he's out for a Sunday stroll, he follows Billy's path. Jerome figures they're in no hurry here, have probably I.D.'d Billy already, don't want to spook him. Only problem is, they get hold of Billy they might want to cut him some slack on this Pawn Shop damage and talk with him about a few other things. Things like if he knows what went down on Wentworth.

Jerome figures it's time to fade away, before the cops get around to asking for witnesses, reconnoitre at the Regal, think this thing out. Later he finds out Billy goes into Denningers, gets himself a coffee and sits down in their little café area, peruses the menu, like he figured he wouldn't look out of place amidst all the well heeled hausenfrau shopping for their swartzbroten and shinklegroob.

Hands in his jacket pockets, head down, walking back along King past the head shops, discount electronics, bars, pizza joints and dollar stores, he crosses James and nips into the mall to get out of the late October chill, just starting to rain. He slows and walks the long way through the mall, not sure of his destination, angry at the recent turn of events. He notices at least half the shoppers in the mall are there the same reason he is, merely seeking shelter, or teenagers on the prowl. As he walks he thinks about that time his Legal Aid lawyer got him to see a shrink before sentencing. He was living with a woman with two little kids back then. Two boys. Actually liked the little buggers. Their mother doing crack when the Children's Services weren't looking, putting out to pay for it, mainly from him actually, but what the hell, a guy's gotta make a living. Not a bad arrangement except he had to look after the kids when their mother was wasted, which got to be most of the fucking time she was into wake and bake. Two boys from two different fathers, didn't look at all alike, one of them, Dylan, probably a little slow on account his mother doing drugs when she was pregnant. The father of Mickey actually taking his boy for the weekend now and then, and paying some support, which didn't make the deal too bad.

But then he pulls a job. A half-assed job. Happened like this, he explains to himself, wandering along the quieter north corridor of the mall, a few shoe stores still open. He hadn't been planning a job, but he'd been getting restless after she gave him shit for letting the boys sit in front of the TV all morning. She was just lying in bed sleeping it off, he tells her, Christ, she could get her own skinny butt up and do what mother's are supposed to do, get the kids breakfast. She says it's her time. "This is my time for myself," she says. She needs it after looking

162

after the little buggers all day. She says "myself" like she's just been to one of those women's self esteem seminars. He points out her so-called "all day looking after them" was really about two hours between seven and nine the night before. She throws a plate at him, screams at him, goes back to the bedroom. The boys sitting glued to the TV keep their heads down, know this is not a time to get into anything. Okay if we watch this cartoon, Jer? They call him Jer. Jerome tells them, yeah, that cartoon's good, and to stay in the house, don't go anywhere, he's going for a walk, maybe bring them back something, a hamburger from McDonalds, how about that?

He wasn't going anywhere in particular, just had to get out of there. It was a Sunday, nothing much going on. He figures he'll just walk it off, maybe she'll be nice he gets back brings her a Qualude. But he's broke at the moment, waiting for her mother's allowance cheque, and it is bothering him, those two little boys, their mother figuring whenever they get into any natural boy mischief they're the spawn of the devil, spend their quiet time dreaming up ways to make her life miserable. He tells her they ain't there yet. They ain't old enough to be conspiring. All they need is a little attention. She says who are you, Dr. fucking Spock? And shit, she's right, he doesn't know anything about raising kids, could hardly use his own mother and father as examples, even if he'd known his father before he graduated to Millhaven on a manslaughter charge. Remembered visiting the old man a couple of times with his mother and little brother in tow. His only image of his father a crew cut stranger behind a wall of reinforced Plexiglas, spider web tattoo creeping up his neck, no interest in his eyes at all for the two boys, only trying to persuade his old lady to meet someone for him, set up a deal on the outside, his mother muttering to them on the way out, "It'll be a cold day in hell before I do that again."

So he wasn't really sure what that feeling was, that feeling he got when Dylan or his little brother Mickey, Dylan a skinny little blonde guy, Mickey darker with almond eyes, came over to Jer asking for a hug, having unsuccessfully tugged at their mother still whacked out on the couch. That warm tingly feeling ran up his stomach. Almost sexual, but not quite. He sure as hell hoped it wasn't sexual, that he wasn't a fucking pedophile. He found that out, he'd off himself.

So that left him, back then, as he walked out of the North End and then up York, with no destination in mind, except to get away, with this confused set of feelings gnawing at him, Dylan and Mickey getting to him, their mother turning out to be a big mistake. The kids were his own he'd sure as hell take better care of them, poor little bastards, all this making him remember when his own younger brother died, drowned at the lake swimming out to the island on a dare, first good day of summer, his mother going all to pieces and the Children's Services putting him in a group home where they tried drugging him with Ritalin again. And he's thinking all these things when he walks by an elementary school.

It was late morning on Sunday, no one around. Most of the Portuguese in this neighbourhood would be in church for another hour or so. And he sees a basement window down the side of the school, a cellar kind of window hinged on the top, slightly ajar, like the janitor had opened it for air and forgot to lock it shut. So he goes for it. It's right there in front of him. Why not? Has to get down on his knees and pull the window up high enough he can crawl through, drop to the floor. He finds he's in some kind of furnace room but it doesn't take him long to locate the stairs and get to the main floor. And, as he already knew, but it's just beginning to sink in, this is a school. He hasn't been in one for years, but it's the same as when he was a kid, a corridor with lockers, what they used to call cloak rooms, the smell of young children like Dylan and Mickey, slightly sweet, a little sour, dirt collectors, small desks and blackboards with big lettering on them, alphabets, cautions like 'look both ways when you cross the street'. It's a school. He says this to himself. It's a fucking elementary school. What the hell is worth stealing in an elementary school? But he's come this far he might as well check out the offices, see if some woman teacher has left a purse behind, or keeping her personal stash of Oxycontin in a desk drawer.

What he didn't know until later was that a couple of non-church going types were out for a Sunday stroll this nice day in early spring, and had seen him crawl in the cellar window. A tall skinny guy, jeans, black baseball cap, maybe a blue top, maybe black, dark anyway, they told the dispatcher at 911, and then again when the cops arrived. For some reason the police arrived in force, three cars, two others on bicycle, been touring the neighbourhood. This school invasion must have been the only major crime so far this Sunday, all these cops available. And as usual, they go over the top.

Jerome's just found one of the offices on the main floor when he's startled by a racket coming from outside the window. He ducks

165

behind a desk but he can see a couple of cops banging on the metal grill, shouting at him to get the fuck out of there, come out the front door, they got cops all around the place. They don't say come out with your hands up, which would be too cowboy even for cops.

Jerome knows there's no way of out of this. He's puzzled by his sense of relief, as he goes back to the main corridor. As if he was holding a party and now he sees his friends arriving and knows everything will turn out as planned. Down the far end the doors are glass and he can see standing outside, waiting for him, is the whole goddamn police department. At least they didn't send the swat team. He's also thinking they get him for break and enter but it'd be tough to prove intent, there being nothing worth stealing in an elementary school.

He gets to the doors, he hesitates for a moment. They're all out there, prancing around, shouting at him, got the batons out, but no guns drawn. He's about to put his hands on his head but that feels foolish and besides, he can't open the doors with his hands on his head, so he just makes sure the cops can see them when he pushes on the crash bars of the first set of doors and then the second, emerging into the sun, casual and harmless, about to say something smart like, "Top of the morning to ya, officers." When they jump him. All of them. Whooping and hollering, they grab him from all around and twist his arm up behind his back and force him down on his knees and then face down on the tarmac. Over the fucking top. You'd think he was Paul Bernardo coming out of a girls' school.

Thing was, to his legal aid lawyer it didn't make sense, breaking into a place nothing to steal. Was it a compulsion? he asked. I dunno, Jerome answered, sitting in the small interviewing room in the Detention Centre, the sound bouncing off the concrete wall. So the lawyer got legal aid to cough up some money for a shrink to visit Jerome and figure this out, maybe get some leniency from the judge, because Jerome couldn't help himself, or some shit like that. Jerome agreed as long as it didn't delay his bail hearing.

The first thing the shrink, a man about mid-fifties, small white beard, said, was, "Man. I hate this place. The constant noise. The colour of the wall. This furniture, the hard chairs. You can't hear yourself think in here. How do you stand it?"

And Jerome said, like the shrink didn't know this, "You got a choice. I don't." And he knew, the moment he'd said it, the shrink was going to jump on it. That phrase: I don't have a choice. The shrink didn't surprise. He jumped on it. Used it to ask about what he called the circumstances of his current arrest, what Jerome had in mind that on fine Sunday morning, what other things he might have decided to do with his time. The shrink kept him about forty-five minutes, making some notes looked like random doodles on the back of a copy of Jerome's charge sheet, and then he summed up, not doing badly in Jerome's estimation, maybe getting some of it right. He told Jerome, "Look, this current charge. Sounds to me you were conflicted, in a situation you wanted out of, you turned to the thing you know best to get you out of it. A break and enter. Gets you back in your comfort zone. I can tell a judge that, but it's not going to do you a hell of a lot of

167

good. The big picture, however (he paused, Jerome figured for effect, looking down at the long rap sheet like he'd never seen it before) the big picture is, you're a career criminal who picked the wrong career. You're just not very good at this."

"I don't always get caught." Jerome told him, feeling a little defensive.

The shrink says, "Even so. You're averaging probably fifty-fifty at best, ignoring the small shit you've been getting away with since your teens. You are simply no good at this. You should maybe think of a new career."

As he emerges from the Mall on Bay, Jerome's so wrapped up in these thoughts, his mind bouncing back and forth between Billy and the big TV and his elementary school B and E, the interview with the shrink, little Mickey and Dylan, his kid brother, he almost gets hit by a car as he crosses Bay in the rain, some big green Touareg driven by a blonde. She pulls up sharp and waves him past. When he settles into a corner of the Regal he becomes aware his hand in his jacket pocket is still gripping the gun. He needs to get rid of it. But he's put out about it. Paid good money to get it, ends up shooting a guy, and nothing to show for it. Maybe the shrink was right. He's just no good at this. On the other hand it's like the shrink's fault he is where he is. The shrink goes off and writes his report, which, later in court, seemed to give the judge a smile, and Jerome remembers thinking, that prick is saying I'm small time, and maybe he has been thinking small, and maybe it's time to go after something bigger. Show the bugger. So in a way, Jerome is thinking, now gulping down a beer in the corner of the Regal, I'm not responsible for this latest thing. He could plead diminished capacity on account of bad psychiatric advice. But here he is, killed a guy, evidence in his pocket, and twenty grand gone wandering. Nothing working for him. He feels a little bad about Dervon. Didn't go into it intending that. But you think about it now, he's carrying and he knows Dervon's not going to be helpful, just give him the money and wish him luck, him and Arlene. The bitch. Jesus. Nothing ever went right for him.

Jerome is on his fourth beer now, deciding it's all about luck, and his luck has got to change someday. Remembers some quote the shrink had used on him without explaining it, just indulging himself, something about a successful man is a man who retains his optimism while he limps from failure to failure. Seemed to be a private joke the shrink was having at the time. I should look him up and ask him to explain. Maybe shoot the bugger, wipe that little grin off his face.

Tilting his head to bring the beer glass to his lips, Jerome sees that Wally is standing in front of him. Just standing there looking at the table which has two more full glasses on it, Jerome having told the girl with the hard body to bring him half a dozen. Wally is just watching the two full beer glasses, his mind grinding slow, a little stooped like a vulture, waiting, aluminum foil peeking above his slim hips.

And Jerome figures he should just shoot him. Pull the gun from his pocket, aim and squeeze, all in one motion, without any hesitation. He wants to shoot somebody. Christ he needs to shoot somebody. Arlene, Albert, that asshole Billy, the shrink. But Wally is the one just standing there, eyes bloodshot, jowls behind a rough shave, giving him that look you wanted to slap, or shoot, or hit with a baseball bat, put it out of it's misery. He plays it in his head. Push the chair back a little using his feet for leverage, to give him room, pull the thirty-eight out of his pocket, one movement, point and shoot. It'd be loud. The bartender and the waitress would just stand there not believing what they've seen. Couple of customers in the back room he notices now, they'd probably keep their eyes down, know enough not to look up. Wally'd probably not know what hit him, just be knocked back a foot, still standing, and then look down at his own belly and see blood leaking all over the foil. Jerome could do this in one straight cut, pull it out, point and shoot, and then casually toss some change on the table and walk right out. Walk out in that loose-limbed Clint Eastwood way. Even better he had a cheroot in his mouth, or paused at the door to light up, like he don't give a shit what anybody thinks.

Man, does he want to do this. He needs to do this. He'd feel so much better he does this. His right hand wants to do this, making the movement already. This Wally with the foil in his drawers needs killing. But it's all about deciding.

23

It's lonely here

In Albert's limited experience he had come to know that there were some times you go after a woman she walked away from you and sometimes you don't. But they didn't come with a playbook, women, so you had to guess which time was which, and, invariably, he'd get it wrong. If it was, say, in a parking lot or on a beach, or downtown Toronto after three in the morning, you could sometimes figure by how far they walked away. If they didn't keep going but stopped less than one hundred yards, then that was a pretty good indication you were expected to walk that hundred yards, apologize in some way, and we're back on track. Or sometimes you go that hundred yards and they go off another hundred yards.

And then the apology. There was no playbook for that either. Explanations didn't cut it. The old politician's, "I didn't mean it that way" or "I'm sorry you took it that way" didn't cut it either. It had to be some kind of outright, "I'm sorry, baby. It was all my fault." But if you did that too quick they might not believe it anyway. He was beginning to think timing was the important thing here. A guy has to wait just the right length of time. Wait too long they figure you don't love 'em enough. Move too fast they figure you haven't been punished enough.

Albert was pondering all this while he lay awake in his childhood bed. He also wondered if Dervon being black was the trouble. So he tested himself. He imagined Dervon being a big white mother-fucking bike-riding drug dealer. Had to give him a whole look to make it fair. A big white guy, worked out, blonde crew cut, fag tattoo on his right pec, pictured in his mind Arlene giving this guy head. He didn't like that either, as much as he didn't like the image of the real Dervon doing it with her. Therefore, he concluded to himself, I am not racist. I'm just a guy doesn't like the thought of his woman doing it with someone else, white, pink, yellow, black, polka dot. So that makes the problem, he reasoned, he was getting into this Arlene. He liked her. He wanted her in his bed. So he should go after her. Maybe enough time had passed. He could use a joint about now, calm himself. He thought about the places in his room he used to stash the stuff. But either his mother had found them all or it was dried up and useless by now.

He remembered the time his mother got him to see a doc when she found him skipping school, marks falling, and he'd just been dumped by some girl. Named Jillian he remembered. First big love. The doc quickly ascertains Albert is smoking marijuana pretty much on a daily basis. He remembered he told the doc that he does it now and then, sometimes. And the doc says, "That 'sometimes' translate to every day?" And Albert answers, "Not really." The doc says, "Does that 'not really' translate to 'almost every day'?" Albert sees it's no use bullshitting this one, so he answers, "Pretty much." "Which might explain", says the doc, "Why your marks are falling, you can't be bothered getting out of bed in the morning."

172

"They're all doing it," he tells the doc. "In school, out of school. Some of them baked all day long still getting good grades."

And then he remembered something he saw on TV, and he asks, "Maybe you could prescribe it for me, you can do that now, eh? Then I don't have to deal, and I could, like, you know, taper off."

And the doc says, "Yeah, it can be prescribed now, for pain, like cancer pain, or nausea from cancer treatment."

And Albert said, "Well, I'm in extreme pain on account of Jillian."

And the doc had laughed and said, "Albert, my boy. You're supposed to feel pain at your age. You're learning about love and loss, and loneliness, and disappointment, and you're learning how to handle them. You stay stoned all the time you won't learn anything."

And Albert, well, he did stay stoned all the time, which may be why something so simple as a well-used woman walking from his bed was troubling him so much. He should go after her. But then you had to factor in something else. She was in the room used to be his sisters. And the very thought of sneaking down the corridor and into his sister's room, with an erection poking out his shorts, was, well, troubling. Like incest. Maybe she'd tell him to get lost, but if his timing was right and she accepted his apology (he knew it wouldn't do any good to tell her of his little trick imagining Dervon as a white guy; that would break the rule he'd figured out, that explanations don't cut it), then they'd be doing it in his sister's room and he was pretty sure he couldn't keep his mind from imagining Arlene being his sister, whose pussy he'd managed to see on one occasion she left the door half open, and was sitting wide legged on her bed. All of which was pretty fucking disturbing.

Albert continued to ponder this dilemma, continued to yearn for a toke or two, threw the blankets off, pulled them back on, went to the washroom, came back, tossed and turned, lay awake all night, but did not go after Arlene.

When Albert came down for breakfast late the next morning, having finally fallen asleep around six, he found the two women had already eaten and were kicking back with their second or third cup of coffee.

"You look rough," his mother said.

"I couldn't get to sleep, maybe too much coffee or something."

Arlene looked at him. She was still minus the tongue and lip ring, looking younger and prettier for it. He tried to read her look, but came up with nothing, maybe, what was that word? Bemusement, like he was a bit of a joke. Not an unkind look, though, maybe forgiving, or maybe she's just enjoying the fact he couldn't get any Goddamn sleep last night. He gave her a weak smile back. He noticed there was no place set for himself, so he had to go get the bowl, the Shreddies, the milk, and a cup for coffee au Carnation. With his head in the refrigerator getting the two percent, his mother pronounced, like she'd been rehearsing this, or had already decided with Arlene, "When you have your cereal I'd like to tell you something."

He sat down, looked at her, glanced at Arlene. His mother waited. He put his cereal in his bowl, then milk, then some sugar, and then he looked at her again. Still she waited, watching him. He looked at Arlene. She was giving nothing away. A white winter light was seeping through the curtains, some traffic noises from outside. His mother said, "This is hard you know. You talk around it all the time, get angry, ignore it, avoid it. Like those families on Dr. Phil. They don't expect him to come right out with it, why they look so surprised." Albert could see her eyes were watery, and he's thinking she's going to tell me she's got cancer or something. But she looks at Arlene and Arlene gives her a little encouraging smile, and she says, "Arlene tells me you've been clean since you got out. So here it is: I'm going to give you one last chance. Both of you can stay here, for the winter anyway. You have to be either working, Albert, you listening? You have to be either working or getting your grade twelve or going to college or something productive, paying some room and board, helping me fix a few things around here. And....And if I catch you using, you're out of here right away, you hear me. One whiff of it and you're out. Okay?"

Albert munched some of his cereal, sipped his coffee. He knew she started in on his using, drinking, giving him ultimatums, shit like that, his surly sixteen year old tended to rise up and argue, even when there was nothing to argue about. He was holding it back. And here she is trusting this Arlene, listening to her more than she'd ever listened to him. Then he heard his mother say, "It'll help me out, as well. The thirty hours I get at Hortons hardly covers the taxes on this place."

He looked up at her. "I didn't know you were working at Horton's."

She said, "You haven't been paying attention. Not for years."

He was trying to picture his mother in one of those sexless brown outfits, the Tim Horton's ladies, either girls from high school, or these older women just covering expenses, calling their customers 'dear', 'honey'. Part-time. No benefits. Hair pinned up, brown cap with a visor. She said, "What was that you said my job was, Arlene?"

Arlene said, "External Customer Interface Manager."

"Right."

"What the hell is that?" asked Albert.

Arlene said, "The girl at the drive through window."

His mother, Gloria, laughed, a relaxed deep laugh, and Albert realized he hadn't seen or heard that laugh for years, maybe the last time being when he was a kid, and his father got amorous for some reason, insisted she come sit on his lap, when they were on holiday. That was it. A cottage on a little lake up near Huntsville. The last time he remembers her laughing. And getting girlish. That was the image. She giggles and sits on his father's lap, and he starts feeling her up, his hand working her skirt up her thigh, and she notices Albert watching and blushes, and the old man laughs at this and tells Albert to go outside and play with himself. His sister is down at the beach with another family with a girl her age. It's a small cottage, really a log cabin, one big living area and a small bedroom. Albert takes his comic book and goes outside, sits on the porch reading. His father takes his mother into the bedroom and Albert can hear them, some laughing, then odd sounds, gentle protests, bed rattling. He remembers feeling impatient with them, bored, he wanted his dad to take him fishing in the boat, but also something else. Was it feeling safe?

It was at that moment the doorbell rang, before Albert had done with this happy childhood memory, before he'd actually answered his mother. His mother, looking surprised, said, "Nobody uses the front door these days, 'cept Jehovah's Witnesses." She took her coffee with her when she went to the door, Albert figuring she thought she'd have to listen to the "good news" for awhile, being much too polite to just turn them away. She'd have to tell them she's a catholic, though not much of a churchgoer these days, not since her husband died, at least that's the way Albert remembered her, always telling strangers too much, the way he saw it, always feeling she had to explain herself, even to these visitors whose "good news" was really that a hundred and forty-four thousand of them were going to heaven, and she was going to hell, come the end of the world. Good News. Them and seventy-two virgins per Jihad martyr would make quite a social gathering, he imagined. He'd like to see their first heavenly get acquainted session, maybe wearing nametags and carrying souvenir bags.

Arlene seemed preoccupied, and he isn't sure what to say to her about last night. The apology he had in mind didn't suit the breakfast table, or the fact she and his mother had obviously been up for hours getting acquainted. It was a surprise, what his mother said, when she came back, though one of those things you know was inevitable, after it happens. Before it happens you just trust to luck, and the world not noticing you haven't paid your electricity bill, or your parking fines, or

177

your account gets credited with too much and you figure you don't say anything you're not stealing and, really, who's paying attention? His mother said, "There's two detectives at the door. They want to speak to Arlene."

24

See the white man dancin'

With his twitching right hand in his pocket, Jerome pushed back from the round table with his feet. In his mind he could see it happening as if he had the bartender's POV: chair slides effortlessly back two feet, his right hand comes up from his pocket with the gun, clears the table with inches to spare, points straight at Wally's belly, grins sardonically, fires. Stands up, tosses his serape over his shoulder, holsters his gun, strikes a wooden match against the table top...

But the wooden bentwood captain's chair doesn't slide. The back legs catch in a break in the old tile, the front legs lift. His right hand rises up quickly. The gun, still in the jacket pocket, doesn't clear the table, smashing his right thumb against a metal edge. With the pain in his thumb, the realization the gun hadn't cleared, and the chair had not moved, Jerome gives a greater push with both feet. At that moment the poor worn chair passes the tipping point, and Jerome feels himself tilting backwards, about to fall. His hands instinctively grab at what they can. And the gun fires.

Recoil from the fired gun completes the chair's journey past the balance point and Jerome goes over backwards. The bullet passes through a piece of foil sticking out from Wally's hip and thuds harmlessly into the old oak bar.

Later, Jerome would replay this scene in his mind and come to the conclusion he was lucky. As satisfying as it might have been to shoot Wally, toss money on the table and stroll out, feeling, if only for a moment, like he was a man to be reckoned with, the long term consequences might have been somewhat limiting.

At the time, Jerome falls back, cracks his head on the tile floor, finds his feet in the air, sharp pain in his shoulders, pain in his right hand, the sound of the gun echoing in the tavern, looking up at the ceiling tiles and sprinkler system, yellowed from years of rising cigarette smoke. He closes his eyes and howls. He tries to curse but the words meld into one long loud howl of anger, anguish and disappointment.

When he opens his eyes he finds the bartender is standing over him, looking down. Jerome knows this guy, an old Russian, keeps to himself, serves the drinks, deals with fights, doesn't drink himself. They call him Boris, though that's not his name. Boris says down to him, "Time go home, Sport. You go now, I forget you have gun."

Jerome pulls himself up, rubs the back of his head. He sees Wally, unperturbed by events, has finished off one of the glasses of beer and is working on the second, sly eyes watching Boris, see if he's going to say anything.

Jerome takes his hand off the gun in his right pocket, pulls himself together, heads for the door. It's not a loose-limbed Clint Eastwood saunter. He doesn't pause at the door to light up, glance back. He steps out on Bay into a cold October drizzle, the red neon behind him. To his surprise he finds himself thinking about Dylan and Mickey, wondering what happened to them, where they are now on this cold wet evening. Back with Children's Services he figures, their mother hooking for crack money. Which means foster homes, and if they raise shit like he did, they go to receiving homes, junior lockups. In the system, poor little Dylan and Mickey. Can we go outside and play, Jer? Is that okay, Jer?

He heads back across Bay to the Jackson Mall to get warm, dry, think about what the hell he's going to do next to get his hands on that twenty grand, turn his luck around. In the mall once was the Eaton Centre, and now houses a department store two points down on the class scale from K-Mart, and several liquidation centres, he's aware of the hole in his pocket, his sore head, the beer swimming in his belly. He buys a pack of smokes, DuMaurier, but knows he can't light up in the mall, and he can't light up back at the Regal. He would have to stand huddled in a doorway. He stuffs the pack in his left jacket pocket and heads through the mall to James. His Civic with the busted window is parked in a lot behind James, a few blocks north, some tickets on it by now. And, he belatedly thinks, probably missing the stereo and speakers. The rain has become annoying, sucking warmth from his shoulders and making everything grey.

When he reaches the Civic he finds the passenger seat and floor are wet, a ticket stuffed under the windshield wiper, and, surprisingly, the speakers and stereo intact. As he takes the ticket from under the wiper, crushes and chucks it, and eases his lanky form into the driver's seat, pushed back as far as it would go, he wonders if the local thieves of opportunity have just insulted him, rejecting his sound system. If he had insurance on his Civic beyond liability he'd take the broken window to his old friend Joe other end of Barton and work out some scam to get an extra hundred for the piece of glass, but he's got no damage insurance. He'd fill the hole with a piece of cardboard, but man, that is so loser, driving around with a beat up car, cardboard where a window should be. So far his day has been such shit he figures he better drop by the little house on Tragina, get himself fixed for the night. And then go home, track down Arlene tomorrow. He is aware he used the word 'home' if only in his mind. The place where he is temporarily residing, he corrects himself. His mother's house in the east end, where he's been living now going on a couple of years not counting his six months in the jail and the trip out west. But he's close to broke and not up to begging tonight so he drives past Tragina. He figures he's still got a little stash in his sock drawer, long as his mother hasn't changed her mind about leaving him alone, trusting God will help him find his way.

Last time he came before the judge, for breaching by going west with Frank and missing his appointments, she showed up in court, bible under her right arm, ready to put up bail money, and the judge, a woman judge, had asked several times, "You sure you want to do this, Ms. Waverly?" And his mother reassured the judge she knew what she was doing, quoted some scripture. Jesus, was it the Prodigal Son speech? He hadn't been listening, concentrating on looking remorseful. And the judge had said, "I'm sure you mean well, Mrs. Waverly, but for your sake as well as everybody else's, I'm denying bail." So back to jail, where he meets the kid Albert, and then he gives this kid Albert the chance of a lifetime, and what doe he do? He fucks me over is what he does.

He was back living with his mother since his release, had to, it was right there on his probation order. Before he turned 18, when they had him in a group home, a social worker would take him to visit his mother between her sessions getting juiced in the Looney Bin, getting her treatments, which he later learned meant a little shot of AC from the wall socket. Even between these sessions she was never quite there, his mother, offering him something to eat, looking him over, then drifting away in her mind, the social worker doing most of the talking. Still they kept the visits up believing it was important a kid know his roots, especially the mother root, figuring you didn't know this you'd have some kind of identity meltdown later, though they didn't really give much of a shit about the father root. Even then Jerome figured that was all bullshit, you are what you do, not where the fuck you come from. After he turned 18 he'd sometimes visit on his own, and crash there for a week or two, depending on circumstances. But what he'd do when he visited his mother, to be honest, was to see if he could borrow money, or find something lying around he could palm and pawn. He never visited her in the Psych Hospital. Who needs it?

Driving through the Junction and heading east on King, the heater in his Civic not keeping pace with the cold wet air coming in the broken window, but causing his feet to be too hot and his Nikes to smell, while his hands and face freeze, Jerome inventoried the day and it's series of fuck-ups, getting himself to the verge of suicide and ready to find a Palestinian and sign up for a little martyrdom going up against the Israelis, bombs hidden in his jacket.

But, you gotta smile a little, he tells himself, thinking about Albert's big screen TV coming through the window and hitting the pavement, and blowing himself off his chair and shooting Wally in the Reynolds Wrap. It's dark by the time he pulls up in front of his mother's house, the porch light on, the old lady probably up watching the Christian Channel on cable, Jimmy Swaggert talking in tongues sounding like Tarzan talking to his monkey, and he's managed to ease himself through the failures of the day and into some optimism. Tomorrow he'll track down that bitch Arlene and his old buddy Albert and squeeze some twenty grand out of them. Still got his 38 in his pocket, minus two rounds. So he ignores the broken window of the Civic and the second chance tonight to lose his stereo, heads up the walk to his mother's front door, thinking, that asshole shrink got it wrong. I'm going to be a successful in my fucking chosen career.

25

Her features covered by her fallen gown

Jerome uses his own key to let himself in, locks the door behind him. The stairs to a bathroom and his bedroom are straight ahead. To his right is the living room, furniture the same from when he was growing up and before his mother was taken up to the hospital the first time. The television is on, his mother sitting in front of it, in her old stuffed chair. She was tall and thin like Jerome, as he remembers her, but she's put on a lot of weight. She says it's the drugs they give her. She looks up at him as he takes his jacket off and shakes it and runs his hands over his black hair. She doesn't say anything. He figures she's taken her pills and is just waiting for them to kick in, before she lies on the couch or goes to the back room. Her pupils are dilated, a bit vacant. Her pill bottles lined up on the small table by her chair, with a glass of milk. He looked them over once, considered pocketing a few, but the only one with any value on the street was a pam drug, clonazepam. The other shit had no value. Seroquel, Lithium, Effexor, Lamictal. His mother doesn't say anything, just keeps her eyes on him for a second and then turns back to the TV, where some guy looks like a closet fag is saying, Jesuuus this, and Jesuuus that.

Jerome says, "Hi mom." And turns away. There's a musty smell coming from the living room. He knows if he tries to talk with her he'll get angry about the smell, the dirty dishes lying around, the empty refrigerator, her failure to bathe as regularly as she should, and he knows this would be unfair. When she bailed him out she had energy, a light in her eyes, a conviction that if she simply cared for him he would find the path of righteousness. That if she gave him a bed, some food, a little love, Jesus would do the rest. Lately she's lost that energy if not that conviction. She sits dumbly in front of her small television set watching game shows, soaps, and 100 Huntley Street. He climbs the stairs to the second floor and its short narrow hallway, the same flower print in a brown frame hanging there on the landing, the left upper corner slipped down. The small bathroom at the end of the corridor has a tub with plastic curtain, a small toilet and single sink. There's a two-piece downstairs that his mother mostly uses.

After a few minutes in the bathroom he goes to the bedroom he's been staying in. He's aware it's looking more and more like a teenager's bedroom with clothes on the floor, pop cans, pizza boxes, unmade bed, though there's nothing pinned to the walls. He picks up one of the empty pop cans, a diet coke can with a small hole punched in the side at the bottom, and pianos in a drawer for a piece of crack left behind, and a bit of steel wool. He sits back on the bed, puts his small find on some steel wool stuffed in the puncture, lights it, and inhales through the top of the can held horizontally. He burns his finger with the match, and a small hole in his pants when he drops the match, and on his second inhalation he burns his lip on the heated pull-tab. A string of profanity ushers from his mouth, and he's about to slip back into feeling like the biggest fucking loser around, when the smoke reaches his brain and nothing matters anymore. Except maybe getting that twenty grand from Arlene, setting up a little lab in his mother's kitchen, and turning twenty grand's worth of cocaine into a hundred grand's worth of crack, keeping a little back for the house. The last thing he hears before he slips away is a sudden rise in volume on the TV downstairs, and the closet fag evangelist shouting, "Rubba rubba rubba. Praise Jesuuus."

26

You'll see the woman hanging upside down

Arlene gets up, says, as if to reassure Albert's mother, "It's okay. I know what it's about."

Gloria waits until Arlene has gone past her, then she sits at the kitchen table, absently reaching for her coffee cup, and holding it. She looks at Albert. He has some of his father's features, but not many. His hair and complexion are light, from her Irish side, but he has his father's broad face, high forehead. He has his father's dark Polish eyes.

When she was honest with herself she realized she was mostly angry about the way her husband had killed himself, not so much the fact that he had done it. He had changed from the man she first knew and married, the drink hitting him quickly, turning surly on a dime those last few years. The steel company had warned him, ordered him into rehab, but he'd injured his back and gone on disability, and then fought with WCB, and the insurance company. He had passed out on the couch most nights mixing alcohol with Percocets. She told herself she had tried to get him help, tried to get him to talk with someone, but she had begun to realize the only time she breathed easily, felt safe, were the times he went out to a bar, or strip joint, or simply the corner store. Her daughter had escaped in the usual fashion, latching onto an older boy, adopting his family as her own. Then Albert escaped into a marijuana haze and she, looking back, waited for the inevitable, while her doctor prescribed for her enough Valium and Paxil to get through the day. Six years ago. They were all victims of his death. Only when she had let herself become hatefully angry at him for doing this, and doing it the way he had, had she begun to breathe, and notice the birds in the back yard. And only in the last few days, with the possibility of her son staying clean, building a life, had she found herself feeling, in the cold November mornings, with the coffee brewing, the radiators heating, the CBC morning show in the background, cosy. That was the simple word, cosy.

Her eyes had been on the coffee cup. She looked up. Albert said nothing. She said nothing, until Arlene returned.

Arlene said, "I'll grab my coat. They wanna take me down to the station to look at some pictures, give them a statement. It's nothing. I'll be back by lunch time."

When she had gone, Gloria turned to her son and asked, "Do you know anything about this?"

Albert considered feigning ignorance. He had been good at it, with years of experience putting a very sincere tone of voice on "I swear to God." "I don't know how that got there, honestly." "I haven't been near your purse. You probably spent the twenty on something and don't remember." "Sure I smoke a little marijuana but I don't go near chemicals."

He opened his mouth to speak, but nothing came out. No denials. No stories. Not even a protest that this was all a surprise to him. I swear to God.

His mother watched him struggle, and she felt anger rising within herself, about to erupt in recriminations, accusations. But then

189

tears came to her eyes and her voice left her. The tears ran down her cheeks. She felt short of breath. She gulped air and felt her body shudder. She looked away from him and sobbed, her chest suddenly hollow.

Albert got up from his chair, stood behind his mother and held her, awkwardly at first, and then easily, his head down beside hers, his arm fully around her shoulder and across her chest. He closed his own eyes and stifled the words that came to him, the words of habit, the words of least resistance: it's not what it looks like. It's no big deal.

She said, when the sobbing eased, "He tucked you in bed every night when he worked days, until you were, I don't know, five or six. And most nights he sang a lullaby, Brahm's. You and Christine. He had a beautiful voice."

There were paper napkins on the table. She reached for one and dabbed her cheeks, and then as Albert straightened up, blew her nose. She said, "Albert. I want you to sit down and tell me the truth. All of it."

As he moved to his chair considering this, she added, "I liked that girl. Maybe I was wrong. I obviously am not the greatest judge of character. So start from the beginning and tell me the truth."

When Albert had sat, and taken his still warm cup in his right hand, and looked back at his mother, seeing her pull strength from somewhere inside herself, he decided he'd try to tell her the truth. As he opened his mouth to speak he became aware how hard this could be. There was an override in his head. As words rose to his tongue they were assessed and modified by some damage control mechanism. He couldn't disappoint his mother's eyes, have them fade in fear and disgust, have them reflect on himself and the way he saw himself. He started to speak and then stopped in mid sentence. He tried again with his eyes averted, this time getting out, "The black guy, drug dealer, killed over on Wentworth. I was there. And Arlene too. She was living there. That's probably why the cops want to talk to her." When he looked back at his mother he saw she was not flinching, her eyes were still fixed upon him, giving nothing away.

She said, "Go on."

So Albert told her the truth, or at least, a truth, modifying a little here and there the bits that made him feel especially stupid. He said, "Arlene's clean, I'm sure about it. And I think she really wants to get her daughter back, Wave."

His mother leaned back in her chair, took a deep breath and dropped her head with a loud sigh. She said, "I have a shift at Horton's in half an hour. You clean up, make yourself useful, and we'll talk again this evening."

As she got up from her chair and moved past him, briefly putting her left hand on his shoulder, she asked, "Do you love her?" But she didn't wait for an answer.

27

Give me crack and anal sex

Jerome recognized the nature of his headache the moment he opened his eyes. Dry lips, sore tongue, his frontal bone being used as an anvil from the inside. Dehydration. And withdrawal. He wasn't sure how many days had gone by, four, five, since firing his gun in the Regal. He'd slept through most of those days, then hauled himself down to the refrigerator, eaten something, planned to go after his twenty grand, track down Arlene, but first he'd hunt in his sock drawer for another bit, and he kept finding just enough to get off, and then he'd decide the problem could wait another day. His mother had ignored him. By the time he had gone downstairs each afternoon to find food, she was back sitting in front of her television, though she must have gone out during the day to stock the fridge.

This time there was nothing left. He scoured the drawers, looked under the bed, came up empty. Standing in the bathtub he gulped water directly from the showerhead until it turned warm. In the medicine cabinet above the single ancient sink he found an old bottle of aspirin and swallowed the few left in the bottom. The small mirror only showed his head and bony shoulders, the tattoo on his right upper arm that would look much better it had a little muscle behind it.

Back in his room he found some clean underwear in the third drawer down courtesy of his mother, and two clean shirts hanging in the closet, hanging above old shoes and boxes accumulated years ago. Once he had that twenty grand he'd get himself a decent wardrobe.

On the stairs going down he heard the annoying and unmistakable sound of morning television coming from the living room and when he turned the corner he saw her sitting there once again, same chair, same stare. He stopped in the doorway and realized she might not have moved; she might have been there all night, bottles of medicine on the chair-side table, the same glass of milk half full. Maybe she'd gone to bed, slept soundly, gotten up, had coffee, placed herself back in her chair for the day. But her eyes were sunken; there was nothing changed in her dress, and he noticed her right fingers were kneading at the covering of the arm of her chair.

As he stood watching her, wrestling with conflicting feelings of sorrow and a wish to slap her a good one, wake her up, her right hand settled down, and she spoke without moving her head. He thought at first she was speaking to the television, talking back to always smiling Regis and the blonde bimbo, but the words were for him. She said, as if they were bits of information that were somehow connected, "They've arrested a bunch of Muslim teenagers planning to behead the prime minister." And, "Your father got parole yesterday."

As interesting as the first news was, as much as it raised curiosity, disbelief, it was the second item that held Jerome's attention. He said, "What?"

She still didn't look up from the television. She said, "They're full of hate, those children. Something is very wrong with that religion."

193

Jerome stayed in the doorway. "Not that. The other thing you said."

She looked over at him this time. "Your father. He was given parole yesterday. That nice officer, Sam, she called me. To warn me."

Jerome said, "It's been years, for Christ's sakes. He's not my father. He's nothing."

"Maybe so," she said, and turned back to Regis.

"Jesus Christ," he said, grabbing the remote from her pill table and pushing the power button. He was distracted for a second by the flickering centre screen flare on the old RCA. He said, "That is a shit television."

She said, defeated, "He is your father. He was your brother's father too. And the last time he was out, you don't know this, you were God knows where, he stayed here. I took him in. He wasn't drinking no more. He'd given himself to Jesus. At least that's what he said."

Jerome sat in the other chair to take this in, looking across at his mother and behind her to the old tri-light, and the framed photograph on the wall of two young boys, him and his brother. The photographs were separate head shots, but framed together, held together for eternity.

She said, "All he wanted was sex. Day and night. Constantly. He wanted anal sex. I told him no. But he did it to me anyway, when I was asleep. I'd wake up with him on top of me, holding me down. You don't know anything of what I've been through."

"Christ almighty," said Jerome. "Too much information. Jesus. I don't need to hear this."

"I was relieved they picked him up for possession again, breaching parole. I was relieved, can you understand that, I was glad he went back to prison."

Jerome is trying to reconcile the images in his head. His bible thumping mom, old, saggy, pepper and salt hair, those sunken eyes, and this man humping her from behind. He shook it clear. "Okay," he said. "So the bastard gets out. So what. He'll probably be at the half-way house, lockdown every night. Nothing to do with us."

"He may come around."

"So don't let him in this time. Call the cops if you have to." He'd said the latter sentence without thinking, regretted it. "Just don't let him in."

"That's easy for you to say." She picked up the remote from the table where he had left it, pushed the power button. Regis came back on, the horizontal control struggling at first, the voice coming before the picture stabilized. They were discussing dieting, Zone dieting, eating the right things at the right time.

Jerome said, his mind having flipped back to the first news item, "They oughta take the little fucks out and shoot 'em."

"That's not very Christian," said his mother, watching Regis and the Zone diet person yuk it up.

He didn't think he'd recognize this man who had donated a few chromosomes to his becoming, twenty-eight years ago, donated them to this woman sitting here hiding in the little screen. He had to get out, do his business, get the hell away. He had reached for her clonazepam bottle, shaken a couple into the palm of his hand, before he said, "Okay if I borrow a couple?"

She behaved as if she hadn't noticed at first, and then, still staring at the screen, said, "You'll do what you want, anyway."

He felt light going out the front door but figured he shouldn't be carrying the piece around. For now it was safely tucked away in his underwear drawer. He could come back and get it once he'd located Albert. His mother didn't look like she planned any laundry today, and even if she found the gun she'd just leave it there, ignore it. He needed to get away, but he stopped himself on the porch, went back in, made some tea and toast, and delivered them to his mother's pill table, pushing the large bottle of Seroquel aside. He said again, "Just don't let him in he shows up."

She said, "Would you believe he's seventy-five years old?"

As he left, Jerome realized his mother was referring to Regis Philbin, not his father.

28

I've heard their stories, heard them all

He said, "So?"

She said, taking her coat off, "So nothing."

He said, "It can't be nothing. Tell me what happened."

She said, "I didn't get anything to eat. Let me grab something and then I'll tell you all about it."

Albert followed her into the kitchen where she halved an English muffin and put it in the toaster. He said, "Last night. I'm sorry I said what I said."

As she found the butter and a bottle of jam she said, "What did you say?"

"You know, I was shitty about Dervon."

"You were jealous," she said, turning to him with a flirty smile, head cocked.

Albert knew it was time to keep his mouth shut. He waited until she had her muffin on a plate and then sat with her at the kitchen table.

Between mouthfuls she said, "They made me wait. They'd talk to me for a few minutes, then go out and leave me sitting there, see if I'd get nervous or something. I gave your mother's address to the Children's Services, that's how they tracked me down."

"Okay. I'm getting nervous. Just what did they ask and what did you tell them?"

"I told them I left two weeks ago on account of the Hell's Angels harassing Dervon. They were threatening him and I figured sooner or later they'd put him out of business, which is all true, by the way. It fit right in with what they knew, so they bought it. And it would have for sure happened that way if Jerome hadn't shown up."

"What about the thing of leaving two weeks ago? Won't they check up on that?"

"I told them I came here and your mother took me in, that I'd known her from the time I worked in Timmy's."

"Jesus," said Albert. "They'll probably ask her about that."

Gloria found most shifts at Tim Horton's quite pleasant. It was warm, busy, the customers usually polite. They liked being called dear and hon, while she fetched their double doubles and boxes of Tim Bits and Dutchies. The time went by quickly and the only true irritant on the job was one younger woman, hair tucked up under a jaunty brown visor, but a constant put-upon scowl on her face. Otherwise, she told herself, it's good therapy. Took her mind off her problems.

But this shift she couldn't get her mind off the current problem and she made a few mistakes, especially trying to fill some of those peculiar coffee preferences like "large, with one-half of the cup two percent milk and four sweeteners, and double cupped please."

At least three times while pouring coffee and refilling the basket, and making change, she arrived at the sensible conclusion that she would have to ask them to leave. They had lied to her, or at least not told her the whole truth. Zero tolerance had become her new policy, thanks to Al Anon meetings, as of a year ago. But....

Albert looked better than she had seen him for several years. He was clean as far as she could tell. Arlene might be very good for him. And, the real troubling part, the last couple of days, sharing the breakfast table, watching her son clean up afterwards, talking with Arlene, sleeping at night with these two kids in the house, actually getting seven, eight hours sleep - this had given her a feeling she thought she'd lost forever. Something bordering on contentment. That cosy thing. So, she decided, she would read the riot act to them but give them another chance.

Or throw them out on the street. Period. "I'm sorry, was that three sugar, one cream?"

When she got home from her shift, seven-thirty, feet sore, legs tired, hungry but not ready to face a kitchen, she found supper on the stove, the table set. Arlene said, "Go have yourself a warm bath. Supper will be ready in half an hour."

Gloria did as she was told, delaying her many questions. Albert asked her, as she went by the living room, "How was your day?" in a voice that sounded practiced, or practicing. She paused for a fraction of a second but continued upstairs to the bathroom, and turned on the taps to fill the tub, for a second adjusting the temperature and breathing deeply of the steam. Her father had often used the phrases, "Let sleeping dogs lie." And "Can't we just let well enough alone?". Probably trying to avoid an argument with her mother. He walked the sunny side of the street. Her mother liked to gnaw at the bones.

The folks at Al Anon didn't think much of avoidance and denial. But who could possibly get up in the morning without at least a little help from these two old friends. The coroner had kindly ruled "accidental death", even with the way he had done it, in the living room….. She had kept her benefits, his pension, had the remaining mortgage erased, given him a church funeral. She added a few drops of oil and eased herself into the water, sinking down until her breasts floated, pushed the unwanted images from her mind.

When she came down dressed in sweats, she found platters of food on the table, baked potato, meatloaf, green beans with almond slivers, and a lit candle. She sat in her usual chair and looked over at Arlene and then Albert. They had waited for her. Albert cut the meatloaf; Arlene served the beans. Some light jazz was coming from the other room, one of the cable music channels. Gloria took a mouthful of the meatloaf, raised her eyebrows and smiled at Arlene. Then she put her knife and fork down, sat back in the chair and said, "All right. Look. Both of you. I hate lying. I simply hate it. I've decided I don't want to hear about the thing on Wentworth, your trip to the police station, drugs, debts, any of it. I wouldn't know what to believe anyway. "

Albert began to say something, but she cut him off. "No. Don't say anything. Please. Let me finish. I'm willing to pretend this is day one. The beginning. I don't want to hear what's been happening because I don't want to be lied to. That goes for both of you. Albert, you look healthier than I've seen you look in five years. I'm fifty-four.

I don't know what that's got to do with anything, but I am. I work shifts at Tim Horton's. I have a few friends. That's it. I would like to have some family."

Gloria lapsed into silence. She wasn't sure where she was taking this. Looking at Arlene, she said, "Your meatloaf is very good."

"I remembered how my mother used to make it," said Arlene. "I just added a lot more garlic."

29

It ain't going any further

It was colder today, a few flurries under a dull sky, the wind blowing scraps of paper up James. Jerome stood across the street from the entrance to the apartments above Faema as long as he could stand it and then went for warmth and espresso at the Five Star. He took up his post again, and waited, shoulders hunched, leaning against the brick. He took another break, this time getting a shot at the bar used to be the Gathering Place, wood oven pizza and Frank Sinatra all day long, until Johnny Pops got blown away in the parking lot a few blocks over, and the new owner found himself at the wrong end of a baseball bat. He heard the whole story in the Detention Centre a few years back, always made him feel better. These guys, the mob, the mafia, were no better at their chosen profession than he was. The shrink could stick that in his pipe and smoke it.

Back at his post watching, he smiled as he retold the story in his head how the brothers had hired a cocaine addict to whack Johnny Pops, to be paid ten grand and another ten in product he managed to do Johnny's Niagara lieutenant as well. The guy drives to the house in Niagara, parks in front, goes up to the front door and rings the bell. Johnny's guy, weighing in at 350, answers the door. The shooter pushes past him into the hallway of the house, turns and shoots Johnny's guy. Johnny's guy falls dying against the front door, blocking it. He's too heavy. The crack head can't move him to get out the front door. So he goes out a window in the living room. He pulls it open and slides his sorry ass out, gets in his car and heads west on the QEW. Couple of miles away he thinks about it, how he opened the window, held onto the window sill, touched the window, left the window open. Cops would see this and dust the glass and the sill. He pulls off the highway. He was supposed to be in and out, touch nothing. His prints will be in the system from the job he did a couple years back. He goes off on a Grimsby side road, cuts across the highway, and heads back to clean up after himself, and he pulls into the driveway just minutes before the cops arrive. When he's collared he gives up the Musitano boys. The shooter gets life. They get a few years. Which tells you two things. One is, it's better to order the job than actually do it, and two, compared to these assholes, Jerome Waverly is a genius with a great future.

Early afternoon he was about to give up, head back to the Regal to think up plan B, when a cab pulls up, and first Arlene gets out, and then Albert, and then that old bastard Billy bust up, now with his right arm in a sling. Jerome waits until they've entered the building and climbed the stairs. Then he crosses over James, almost getting taken out by an SUV heading north, because he's forgotten it's now two-way, after years of being one-way. Those one-way streets being real good you wanted to flee a crime-scene or otherwise get the hell out of the city. He takes the time to raise a middle finger at the SUV driver, and then steps onto the sidewalk by the display window of stainless steel pasta makers.

Harry was out of breath by the time they reached the landing on the second floor. Albert opened the door to Harry's apartment and stood aside for Harry to enter. Harry stopped. He said, "I think it's a little overdue for a major cleanup."

Arlene's words, seeing the piles of books and papers and the narrow passageways between them, were, "Naw. Give it a couple more years, this shit will turn into oil and we can sell it."

In the kitchen she suggested that Harry use the stove and fridge while they watched, made sure he could manage with his right arm in a sling. Harry was demonstrating, unsuccessfully, the opening of a can of tuna, when the door to his apartment, left open, suddenly slammed shut.

Jerome appeared in the doorway of the kitchen, shook his head, said, "What a fucking dump."

Albert had been worried about Jerome, but they figured they could bring Harry home, get in and out quick, and the odds he was watching the building that closely were pretty small. But obviously, not small enough. Albert assumed he was carrying a gun. Harry sat in a kitchen chair, ignored Jerome, turned his attention back to the can of tuna.

Jerome had rehearsed this in his mind, the moment he found Albert or Arlene. But with both together in that small kitchen, the old man curiously fumbling with a can opener, what he said was, "Now isn't this fucking cosy." He was conscious of not carrying his piece. Sure he could inflict damage on the two of them, or the three of them, but that wasn't the point, was it?

And Albert, who had considered many responses when Jerome caught up to him, including running, arguing, and denial, said, calmly, "We have the money and we're prepared to give you your third, after damages like my TV. A third should come to around six thousand."

Harry looked up. He had managed to lock the opener in place and had cut a centimetre slit in the top of the can of Albacore. "You fractured my elbow for six thousand dollars?"

Arlene was looking at Albert, mouth half open. Jerome ignored Harry, said, "Albert, my son, I don't know how this came off. I don't know you knew this whore before or not. It's a puzzlement. But I know where you live, where your mother lives. I even know where Arlene's little girl Wave lives. So you are going to give me the whole amount. You got it on you now or we go to where it's at."

Arlene leaned back against the counter in a pose Albert recognized from somewhere. She said, "Jerome, sweetie, there wasn't much to it. Dervon hadn't been doing so good. The total was just over five thousand and I believe we've gone through most of that, and given the rest to Albert's mother."

Jerome said, "That is such horseshit. Arlene, baby, you do take the cake. You got so many stories on you, you oughta write for Law and Order." He was standing in the doorway to the kitchen. Harry remained sitting. Arlene and Alfred were standing on the other side of the table, backs against the counter, sink, refrigerator. It was a very small room. Jerome regretted not bringing his piece, remembered his plan to find them, go back and get the gun, not carry it around all day, but have when he confronted them. He'd skipped the 'go back and get it' part. Now he wanted to just beat the crap out of all three of them, except maybe the old man, who was merely annoying, pretending to ignore everything but his can of tuna. Albert didn't look so tough, but three of them in this small space, he wouldn't get very far. He took a chair, straddled it. This would be a good moment to light a cheroot, tilt his Stetson back on his head, stare at them. The old man finally got the lid off the can of tuna, dumped the contents on a plate and said, "Voila."

Jerome stared at them. He said, "Here's the deal. I'm tired of running around town looking for you. So I'm going to give you an address. You deliver the whole twenty grand by seven this evening, we're square. You don't show I come after you and your momma. You got it?"

Harry said, "You know how much mercury they say's in this tuna? Ten parts per million. You eat this every day you start to glow."

Jerome looked at him. Harry went on. "Mercury in the fish, carcinogens in the air, global warming, cities in decay, Islamists blowing up anybody they don't like, a whole continent dying, Mr. Bush threatening to go to war again." He looked up at Jerome. "This young man and this young woman, they've been good to me. You harm them you're going to have to deal with me."

Jerome laughed. He squinted first at Harry, shook his head, and laughed. "Holy fucking shit, Albert, you got a senior citizen watching your back."

"What I'm saying," Harry went on, unperturbed, "Is that there are some big things to think about and you, sir, are not one of them.

206

Leave the address and let me enjoy my fish." And to Albert, "See if there's some lemon pepper in that cupboard, and a little olive oil."

Albert found the spices, olive oil, some crackers, and added a knife, fork and napkin for Harry. Harry worked at his concoction, mixing in the olive oil and lemon pepper. He had trouble spreading it on a cracker. Arlene sat down to help him.

Jerome watched this. He didn't know what else to say or do. Not without a gun to wave at them. He knows that if he repeats himself it begins to sound weak. So he simply says, "Give me a pen, I'll write down the address."

Albert found one on the counter and obliged. Jerome wrote down his mother's address. He said, "Seven o'clock. You bring the whole lot, all of it, I don't hurt your mother, or your kid. No. I'm not telling it straight. I couldn't hurt a kid. You, you cunt, I could happily cut you up, and Albert's mother. But not the kid. That's just the way it is. I got standards."

Harry said, "This is always good. A little lemon pepper and olive oil. I get the oil right across the street at the Portuguese fish place. Better than virgin. Virgin they've taken all the flavour out."

"Jesus shit," said Jerome. "I should break your other arm. Albert, you heard what I told you, you believe it, you just nod once."

Albert nodded, said, "I believe you'll do what you say."

Jerome got up from the chair. This had not gone the way he imagined it. He needed to punctuate his declaration. He needed to spit on the table, stub his cheroot in the old man's tuna. He settled for swearing some more and pushing over some piles of books and papers, two chairs, and clearing a new path for himself. He went out the door and slammed it shut.

Jerome hoped he'd scared them enough, they'd bring the money over to his mother's. With that twenty grand he'd start fresh in Calgary. Or maybe wait until spring. Jerome stepped into the pawn shop two blocks up James, fished in his pocket for the gold ring he'd found in his mother's dresser, got a few bucks for it, the price of gold being at an all time high. It was a man's gold ring. He wondered if it had been his uncles, or even his fathers, and what was the old lady holding on to it for? He was convinced she'd never notice it was gone, and if she did notice, she and her new buddy, Jesus, would forgive him.

With the money he got for the ring he walked back down James to Barton, went west a block and a half, then picked the one house in a row of two and a half story semis, the one with an American flag covering a broken second story window, garbage on the porch, for sale sign on the small front yard. He climbed the three steps to the porch and knocked on the door. A pimply-faced kid opened the door a crack, then let him in quickly, shutting and bolting behind him. Let him in much too quickly in Jerome's estimation, figured one glance he could tell Jerome was not undercover, like it was that easy. The kid, out of the shadows, looked older, but there was a real kid, looked maybe four or five, playing on the floor just inside the door, vrooming a hot wheels car back and forth. The guy who let him in, bleary eyed and stoned, was doing the wassup dude, and my man and dawg jive, between sucking it in between his thin lips with the wispy moustache.

Jerome said, "You shouldn't smoke that shit around the kid."

The guy, as thin as Jerome, but shorter, stayed cool, looked at Jerome a little closer, said, "You with the fucking Children's Aid or you here to score?"

Jerome said, "It's cool. You wanna raise a moron, you raise a moron. I don't' give a shit."

'It's not like it's tobacco for Christ's sakes. You here to buy or you here to stick your nose where it don't belong?"

Jerome shrugged. The house was a dump, kinda damage you get with ten young guys randomly bunking down with dope, gangsta rap, video games and some chicks can't do any better. And making babies on the side. When he was looking after Mickey and Dylan he didn't smoke nothing in front of them, least he didn't blow it in their direction. He took another look at the kid, who was still making noises but hadn't said a word. Should be talking by now, and walking, not dragging his full diapers across the ruined floor. The place smelled of some unpleasant combination of weed and urine. He could hear the tinned gunfire of video games coming from the next room.

He fished the money from his pocket, told the kid he wanted some good quality weed and some E or 'shrooms, whatever. The kid took the money, climbed the stairs to the second floor, leaving Jerome with the child. Jerome was thinking this is the kind of scene he's gotta get away from. Gotta get himself set up properly, get some distance between himself and his own dealers, live in a high rise, share his bed with a woman wasn't addicted. The child on the floor reminded him of Dylan, happy to play alone he wasn't being hit or yelled at. The child looked up at him. Jerome couldn't help himself, gave the kid a big toothy grin. The kid smiled back. Probably a little stoned, there was so some much cannabis in the air.

Jerome was happy to see the guy return from upstairs, a couple of zip lock bags in hand. The kid at his feet was gnawing at him. He wanted out of there. He took the bags and walked past the kid, down a hallway, through a kitchen, dishes and food and garbage all over the place, full sink, table littered with old pizza boxes, unbolted the back door and stepped out on a rotten porch. He hadn't checked he wasn't being ripped off; he had bigger fish to fry tonight.

The sun had gone down. It was colder. A few flurries coming off the lake. When he got back to his Civic, crumpling and throwing away another ticket, he took a couple of the tablets from the freezer bag and washed them down with the cold remains of a double double sitting in the cup holder from the morning. It was hard to make out the tablets in the dusk. He didn't want to turn the car lights on and draw attention. The tablets might have been purple, maybe closer to pink in a good light, an imprint on one side he couldn't read. Laced with something he hoped was good. Find out soon enough. He looked at his watch. Time to get home, chill a while and wait for Albert to bring him his money, which Jerome was sure he'd do after he thinks about it awhile.

****

Nobody said anything for a few minutes, Albert standing, Arlene sitting, helping Harry with his tuna and oil. Finally Harry gave

210

up on his snack, said, "I think the question you have to ask yourself is, is this man capable of carrying out his threats?'"

"Yeah." Said Albert. "But I think we know the answer."

"Definitely." Said Arlene.

"I assume you can't go to the police."

"Not a good idea," said Arlene.

The light was fading. Some flurries of snow scratched against the small kitchen window. Harry went on, "So then you have to ask yourself if this money is worth someone's life."

"Gotta be another way of dealing with it," said Albert.

"Ah, my young friend, the way I see it, you can smoke a little weed, drink some Rum, pretend it isn't happening, or you can visit some of the boys in the neighbourhood, see if you can get that fellow whacked for twenty thousand, or you can give him the money, and read some poetry."

Arlene said, "Read some poetry?"

"Not literally, my dear. I'm just trying to point out there may be more important things in life."

Albert joined them at the table, taking the last of three kitchen chairs. They sat in silence for a minute. Arlene said, "He'll be back we don't show up tonight."

Albert looked across at Arlene. In the fading light she was beautiful, though he knew enough to not tell her that, not in those words. They had a place to live. If they both worked. The money and Jerome still connected him to Dervon. He looked up at the clock on the wall. He said, "We've got just enough time to get back to the house, get the money, and deliver it to Jerome by seven."

Arlene said, "It really burns my ass. Can we short him or something?"

Albert said, "He thinks there's twenty grand. We can keep a couple thou."

Harry said, "I'm coming with you." As they considered this, he added, "Albert, it's time we all made a new start. I know you watered down the booze more and more at the hospital."

"You knew I was doing that?"

"Yes. So I'm sober and I won't go into withdrawal. My daughter might take me in if I stay sober. And you two. You, if I'm not mistaken, rather like one another. You can have a life together. You don't need this money." Not that Harry wasn't trying to think of a way that some or all of the twenty thousand might come his way. Perhaps his friend from the hospital, Donny, might be able to help. But that would be Donny as a younger man, ready to mix it up with the likes of Jerome. They were both too old for this now. So, all things considered, it would appear that his age and circumstances would force him to do the right and moral thing. Maybe he should settle for writing a poem. While youth, he remembered, as G.B. S. once said, is wasted on the young, it might also be said, that age is wasted on the old.

212

30

The breaking of the ancient western code

He couldn't trust Arlene, but Albert he was sure, would see the light. Albert was a pussy. He would show with the twenty grand, all nervous and shit. He had it to do over he'd do the Wentworth job on his own. But, there was something about the kid. As he turned onto King at the junction, loose ends gnawing at him, Jerome fished in the baggy of pills in his pocket and re-upped, swallowing another with his own saliva. His younger brother, Justin, would be Albert's age about now, had he lived. Silly bastard. He could see the lake in his mind, that first summer day, everyone lying around smoking dope, Jerome's mind fixed on Alex. Alex she called herself, lying on her front in the sun, top off, giving him a flash now and then, so he wasn't paying much attention when his little brother decides to swim to the island and back, off his Ritalin since the old man was sent up, and his mother working extra hours. Time in a haze, a couple of guys showing off, swimming out after Justin, then standing on the island maybe a couple hundred yards off shore, shouting at them, horsing around, and then gone, maybe on the other side doing who knows what, while he's showing Alex how to make a bucket from two plastic bottles, a straw, and some lake water, taking it behind some bushes, where he also hoped to cop a feel or two. He remembered the haze taking over, the warm fuzzy touch, sand and grass, Alex's fine tits, and not realizing how late it was

213

until the other swimmers came back, the sun dipped below the tree line, and somebody asked, "Where's Justin?" And Jerome pulls himself up, concerned about the big wet patch on his trunks, jumps in the lake to hide this, comes out dripping wet, getting cold, looks at the two swimmers, towelling off, says, "Where the fuck's Justin? You assholes leave him out there?"

"He was swimming back," says one of them. "Maybe he's on the other side, fooling around."

A wind was coming up when they all stand there on the shore calling to him, calling him "Justin, you asshole." And Jerome finds himself getting scared. One of the girls says they should get a boat to go look for him. Another says they should call 911 or something, but they gotta get rid of the beer bottles and bongs first.

They find a rowboat and Jerome rows out to the island with Alex, still thinking, with any luck, they'll find Justin swimming back and he can continue to the island with Alex who's pretty wasted, and then find a nice patch of soft grass and get lucky. By the island it gets colder in the shadows of the trees, the wind picks up, and they run aground in a tangle of weeds. When Jerome pulls the boat up on the muddy sand, beginning to realize he is not going to get lucky with Alex, who is shivering, they look back across the lake and see police cruisers and a rescue van pull up in the field behind his friends.

His mother didn't say anything directly but he knew she blamed him. He should have been watching out for his kid brother, off his Ritalin and into everything, afraid of nothing. Then she stopped going to work, just sat in her chair, much like she's doing these days, until the ambulance took her away and they stuck him in a group home.

He wasn't sure why he was thinking about all this while he drove down King East in the direction of Stoney Creek. Depressing shit. He'll be rid of all of it soon, with twenty grand in his pocket. He could feel his pulse rising, headlights getting sharper.

By the time his Civic pulled up in front of his mother's house, Jerome was feeling the first rushes of ecstasy. You could sometimes tell what was in the tablet along with MDMA from the quality of the zoom, some easy love with Heroin added, a donkey's kick with cocaine, but as Jerome felt the steering wheel squirm under his fingers, his heart thumping in his chest, his mind flying with the snow flakes, his ears popping, he couldn't tell. Street lamps were magical, bare branches glistened with new ice. He was king of the fucking world.

How many had he taken? He had a moment's doubt about the wisdom of re-upping before seven tonight, but it was a done deal. He was on the E train. He wanted to get inside, get past his mother quickly, up to his room, where he could rub his aching balls, shave his body, roll in some silks, get the money, go out and get laid.

He opened the front door with his key. The television was on. He turned to tell her to call him when his friends arrived, but she wasn't sitting in her chair. As usual some plump well-dressed moron was going on about his friend Jesuus, but nobody was watching. The other

215

thing he noticed it was hot in here, in the house, the furnace working overtime, like she bumped it up to thirty or something. He would ignore this in his rush to get to his room, do his business, but for the sound of plates or glasses being shattered against the tile floor in the kitchen.

There was something he knew he should remember, but his mind was cascading between fear and euphoria, awhirl in serotonin and memories, circuits on overload. He went past the steps to the second floor, down the small hallway toward the kitchen with calls for "Jesuus" at his back.

She was on the floor in the corner of the kitchen, next to the refrigerator. Her nose was dripping blood down her chin, onto her blouse. An eye was swollen shut. The other eye was blank. She was sitting there, arms at her side, hands softly open on the floor. And a man was sitting across from her, the other side of the small kitchen table, a twenty-six of something in front of him, right hand holding it. Jerome noticed the back door was broken, shattered around the lock and handle, letting cold air in from the porch. He realized the heat he had felt earlier was coming from himself, not the house, at the same time he realized that this man sitting there, now looking up in his direction, was his father.

It wasn't as if he never felt like hitting her himself, but she was his mother, for God's sake. Now sitting on the floor with the swollen eye, her legs sprawled apart and her hands lolling on the floor palms up.

The man had a shaved head, which might look sharp he was twenty years younger. Tattoos curled up the back of his neck, down his arm around his exposed bicep. Jerome couldn't talk. The chemicals which were, a moment ago, stimulating euphoria, great expectations, were now bouncing in the vault of paranoia. And hatred. And fear.

The man, his father, said, "What the fuck you staring at?"

Jerome was frozen, unable to move. At the same time the muscles in his cheek, his legs, began to twitch uncontrollably. The light in the centre of the ceiling hurt his eyes. His father's voice assaulted his ears. And someone he was sure, was watching all of this, through the windows, the walls. He looked to his mother who acknowledged nothing with her one good eye. He imagined this bald man forcing her over the kitchen counter, pants around his knees, his mother muttering prayers. A lump of rage grew in his chest.

His father took a swallow from his bottle and spoke again, "Jesus shit. Are you on fucking drugs?"

Jerome's legs worked. He passed his father, walked through a shattered plate, and went to his mother, knelt beside her. Her one good eye focussed on him. He said, stupidly, "Are you all right?"

His father, still in the kitchen chair, said, "Of course she's all right. She cracked her head on a cupboard getting something."

His mother said, in a whisper, "That's right. It was an accident. I was getting something. I slipped. I'll be fine."

His father said, "See. What'd I tell ya. It was an accident."

Jerome stood up and faced his father. He said, "That was no fucking accident." His father had that con look about him, the look he'd

217

seen on the hard-timers. Muscles from working out, pale skin, nicotine fingers, sunken wary eyes, a hard caged look. Or the look of a man afraid of his freedom. A man who has grown accustomed to orders and bars, saying yes sir to the stronger, and walking over the weaker.

'You little shit," said his father, rising from his chair. He was shorter than Jerome, who noticed the kitchen clock behind the bald man said six thirty.

"Don't you fucking touch her again," said Jerome.

Then his father said something in that reckless hateful way of his, something best left unspoken. He said, "You little chicken shit. If you weren't such a dope-head chicken shit your brother'd be alive today."

"You bastard," said Jerome, lunging at his father.

But his father had the muscle, and the experience close in. Face to face, screaming at each other, holding on, chairs toppling, it was only seconds before his father had Jerome on the floor, right next to his mother, holding him down on his back. His father said, "It was Justin had some future, woulda made something of himself. You were supposed to look after him."

"You weren't there. You weren't there. You weren't fucking there," Jerome shouted in his father's face, and then the tears came. They came with waves of remorse and flashes of memory, with the rush of ecstasy gone sour. He didn't know he was crying.

It was the tears that caused his father to let go, seeing this man, his son, go red faced, limp, and crying under his grip. He pushed himself up and away like a man retreating from a bad odour.

And Jerome rolled over on his front, across the kitchen floor toward the hall, pulled himself up with a hand on the corner of a counter, and left the room. He could hear his father's mocking laughter following him, and again when he climbed the stairs to his room, and when he opened his sock drawer to get the gun.

It was after six when Sam got out of the office. It was that Mike and Beverlee situation that held her up. Mike and Beverlee and Shawn and Allissa situation. She'd agreed to meet with them and the Children's Services worker, after Beverlee came in pushing on this thing. Mike still had his job. If the court would let Mike come to the house, if the restraining order was lifted, and the terms of his probation were changed, maybe then Children's Services would let Mike have unsupervised visits with Allissa. Mike was pushing for this too, though Sam was pretty sure his interest was not really Allissa. It had to be, let's be realistic here, either he hoped to catch Shawn and punch him out, or screw Beverlee. It can't really be about the kid. Or, that was another possibility, if he got custody and gave the kid to his own mother to raise, by catching Beverlee using or something, then he's free of child support. It can't really be about the kid. The last Goddamn thing this is probably about is the welfare of the child.

The meeting had gone on an hour and a half, with Sam, or so she thought, quite reasonably, asking two clear questions of the Children's Services Worker, "What precisely was their concern about

Mike picking up Allissa and taking her to McDonald's on occasion, and what would they be asking for in court when the current supervision order was over in ten months?" And the answers she got were, that in the first matter, the agency "had concerns" about Mike's parenting skills, and Beverlee's as well, and for the second, "that would depend on their assessment, and would have to be discussed with their supervisor." Sam had to remind herself that they were on the same team here.

Inevitably in the meeting, both Beverlee and Mike stated, at least once each, but not at the same time, "This is so much bullshit." And Sam, though she found some merit in their assessment of the proceedings, understood that their forthrightness would ensure a further six-month supervision order. And so it went. In having the meeting, not only was nothing achieved, but she probably hurt Beverlee's chances of sharing parenting with Mike, or getting money from him, and Mike looked angry enough at the end to quit his job, take off for Alberta, and breach his probation order.

She was tired at the end of the day and didn't really want to make a home visit. But she had promised Mrs. Waverly, who sounded quite fearful on the phone, as well as resigned, flat, and depressed. Sam had called to warn her about her ex-husband's parole a few days earlier, maybe not ex. Maybe still her husband. Going to jail on a manslaughter charge is not an automatic divorce. And today, around noon, Mrs. Waverly had called back, rambling vaguely and fearfully, and Sam had promised to drop by.

It wasn't the right time of day to be driving across town, and she'd never been to this address before, so it wasn't until a quarter to seven that she found the street and then the house, a one and a half story frame from maybe 1950, a light dusting of snow covering the poor front yard.

She parked behind a Honda Civic with a busted window, wondered about it for a second, and then walked up the path to the door. She was on the porch, her finger reaching for the doorbell, when she heard two shots fired in rapid succession.

In the Hamilton Taxi on King East, Arlene had just pointed out it was already ten after seven, when they heard the siren coming from behind them. Albert was in front, Harry and Arlene in the back seat. The cabby pulled over to let the ambulance pass.

Arlene had been talking rapidly, if somewhat circumspectly for the cab driver's ears, about finding a way of keeping all or some of the money, because it wouldn't do Jerome any good, and she needed it to get a fresh start and make a good home for Wave. Harry, in a fatherly manner that surprised even himself, put his hand on hers to quiet her. A gentle pat.

The cab driver was an Iraqi they had learned, Harry asking these kinds of questions of strangers, in Hamilton since, what he called, the First American Invasion of his homeland. Harry had pushed for more. Shiite? Sunni? Kurd? But the driver had changed the subject, told

221

them he had never been to this street before but he was sure he could find it.

When he did find it, and had turned onto it, they saw instantly, a block and a half ahead of them, the ambulance, and three police cars, bubbles still flashing, the pulsing red light dancing with the gentle flurries of snow. At the next intersection they were stopped by a police officer who impatiently waved them to detour, to turn left or right. The cabbie didn't move, thinking this through, while Albert, looking at the house numbers in the first block, quickly calculated that the ambulance and police had responded to the address at which they were to meet Jerome, or at least next door to it. Through the snow, under a porch light, he could make out a woman in a winter coat standing with police, the woman looking a lot like his probation officer.

The cop at the intersection walked slowly to the driver's window, but before the Iraqi had time to say where he wanted to take his passengers, Albert leaned over and said, "We're trying to find the Jolly Cut, to get up on the mountain." The cop ignored him, said to the driver, "Take them back to King. We have a situation here." He backed away, gestured to his left, and the Iraqi turned his cab onto the side street and stopped.

The cabbie looked in the mirror at Harry, "I can let you off here or we go."

Harry said, "Albert, give the man a good tip and then have him take us to the restaurant of your choice. I think we have some celebrating to do. "

222

31

Love's the only engine of survival

Billy was quite pleased to see the iron gate slide open to let Jerome enter the range with towel, sheet, and blanket in his arms. The screw, Laura, said, "We got an old friend back, Billy, don't you lead him astray."

Jerome said, "Can you explain to me, why you went into Denningers?"

The gate slid shut behind him, Laura on the other side. Billy started going on about a new doc at the jail, senile bastard, got him on some good bug juice, and would Jerome like to buy the few he managed to cheek. Jerome looked around, saw some familiar faces. He wouldn't be here long, get himself through the winter, think about pleading out to a light sentence for manslaughter, self-defence, the evidence right there, and his mother, once she got out of the hospital, be willing to say the old man was beating the crap out of her when Jerome come home, only thing he could do was shoot the bastard. No, he'd get off light, a few women on the jury, especially if his lawyer could keep out his priors, and then come the spring…..

That Christmas eve Arlene moved into Albert's room so that Wave could sleep in Christine's room the first time she had been allowed, by Children's Services, to stay overnight. Arlene had taken

223

over much of the cooking; Albert was working on some correspondence courses; the tree was up; Christine reported that she was back with her husband in B.C. and wouldn't be home for Christmas this year, and when she woke on Christmas morning, Gloria allowed herself a few minutes to luxuriate between the sheets, to roll on her back and spread out in a posture of acceptance and vulnerability.

They had coffee au Carnation with croissants and jam while they watched Wave make short work of her stocking. Gloria sat back with her mug and watched Albert watching Wave, seeing in his eyes and in his face, a kindness not there before, at least not since his childhood. Arlene was excited, and had to step outside for a smoke to calm herself. Gloria hoped this was not a sign of impending flight, a retreat from a happiness and contentment she would feel she didn't deserve.

They had invited this man Harry for dinner, Albert assuring his mother that Harry was sober, and Gloria responding that it didn't matter much this one day of the year, so long as he, Albert, didn't fall back into any bad habits.

They cooked a turkey with everybody helping. Harry came with flowers in hand, and old-world courtesy. Albert drank too much; Arlene went out to smoke too often; Harry told Wave fantastic stories about little girls and boys her age; while Gloria, not sure at all what would last and what wouldn't, enjoyed the moment, and went to bed late, after fixing a sofa for Harry to sleep on.

In bed that night, unable to sleep, Gloria did the crossword and read the paper from the day before, mildly curious about the young man awaiting trial for killing his criminal and abusive father, the Crown asking for a long sentence because, they claimed, this man had had opportunity to leave the house and call the police but instead came back with a gun in hand and the intention to commit homicide. Gloria was thinking how much more there must be to this story as she moved on to read about the city councillors voting to erect an enormous fountain in the Harbour to improve the city's image, or build a stadium on the waterfront, or plant more flowers. She put the paper down and turned out her light. For a moment she was sure the voice she heard faintly wafting down the stairs and into her bedroom, was her son's voice, singing for Wave, "Lullaby and good night. In the sky stars are bright. Round your head, flowers gay, bring you slumbers today."

.... And then she fell asleep.

Lightning Source UK Ltd.
Milton Keynes UK
UKOW03f0736030614

232757UK00001B/66/P